ALEX ICICLE

*A Romance in
Ten Torrid
Chapters*

Robert Kaplow

ALEX ICICLE

*A Romance in
Ten Torrid
Chapters*

*Houghton Mifflin Company
Boston
1984*

Library of Congress Cataloging in Publication Data

Kaplow, Robert.
  Alex Icicle : a romance in ten torrid chapters.

  Summary: Fourteen-year-old Alex realizes that his desperate, unspoken love for fellow eighth-grader Amy can only end in tragedy when he learns that her father has been transferred to California.
  I. Title.
PZ7.K1295Al 1984   [Fic]   84-10740
ISBN 0-395-36230-X

Printed in the United States of America

S 10 9 8 7 6 5 4 3 2 1

To Anthony Akey

ALEX ICICLE

*A Romance in
Ten Torrid
Chapters*

1

I am a sick man. I am a diseased man. I am not even a man, merely a boy. *And yet I love her.* I am all the loathsomeness of the human condition distilled into one horrible, malignant growth and fashioned into the fourteen-year-old features of Alexander Preston Sturges Swinburne — boy monster.

Nay, when you read this line remember not the monster who writ it. Burn the wretched manuscript! Obliterate every vestige of its fetid presence from the face of humanity. The contents of this manuscript are so void of redeeming social value, so unspeakably low, so depraved and degrading, that I warn you (pray heed my warning!) to put it down. There are gentle books all around, books with pictures of gardens. There are books of sunlit poetry. Gentle reader, I implore you to read one of these other books, not the horrible document you hold before you. It is a record of humiliation and anguished self-hatred — stop, dear reader! Stop if you dare. Or, at least, hold the manuscript with long steel tongs so it cannot possibly touch you with its poison. But steel tongs may not be enough! Place the manuscript in a containment cell and reach through the walls with long neoprene gloves as your startled, trembling fingers turn each rancid page. But make sure there are no holes in your gloves! Check carefully! Even one pinprick, and the foul and pestilent vapor will creep up with long, dark, gaseous fingers to pull you down into the abyss of degradation.

So read on if you dare, for I know I (crying now) cannot stop writing. I must confess it all! Every word and every hellish thought must be confessed. I cry, I sob, I throw my arms in the air; my head pounds, filled with boiling fever, *but I will not be stopped.*

The doctor by my bedside (I'm making this part up) stares at the throbbing body he sees before him. He shakes his head. If only his professional code would let him escape this nightmare room *(for just one minute!).* But like you, gentle reader, he is locked into this deepening dream of self-destruction for the length of the whole trip. I warned you! I warned him! But, no, they stand with noses pressed to the hospital glass, staring in horror. Behold how their eyes start from their spheres!

2

I love her! (Have mercy on my poor, troubled soul.) Amy Hart! I have said her name. And I have disgraced heaven by uttering it. My lips have pronounced the loveliest of all syllables, and those soft, lyrical sounds have been forever shattered. Amy Hart! The first name is liquid, summer streams; the loop of the capital *A* is wind through the meadow (I've actually never seen a meadow, but I imagine it's something like that); the tail of the lower-case *y* is the fall of a silken scarf, graceful and secret. And *Hart!* First the *H* — all hot and beating, red-blooded — then stabbed to lingering death with the final *t,* an arrow that even now, as I sob by my flickering candle, pierces through the walls I thought I had fashioned and tears at my poor, battered heart.

Amy Hart! Goddess on earth. Fourteen-year-old maiden. O Amy! Unravished bride of Edison Junior High School. The school falls hushed at the sound of those molten, golden tones, dove-wing, silverdust, O Amy Hart! I fall before the temple of your beauty. Do you not feel my thoughts tonight as I sit in the freezing garret of my horror-haunted home, desolate on the Night's Plutonian shore! Ah, nevermore! O Amy —perfect gown of white silk stamped in the black mud, sullied forever by the midnight fever of my desires. I am rotting death, Amy! I am stink-bag of rat feces; I am slime-monster; I am gorilla. Penned and chained, I sweat and roar. But I love you, Amy! Look at me. I weep. I beat my claws in a frenzy upon the glass wall behind which I must stand.

I love you.

I shout it to the thundering masses who riot now at the foot of my castle walls. "Kill the madman!" they shout. "Kill mad Doctor Swinburne!" But no! I stand, bellowing back to the madness of the moon. I madly dance and pull the wild bell rope. The tintinnabulation of the bells! I love her! Did you hear me? I dare to love her! Fire your puny arrows at me! I laugh! I, Alexander Preston Sturges Swinburne (Swine-born! Swine-born!) — with all the groping, hopeless power of my aching soul, my tormented soul — I say, I scream: I love Amy Hart! I love her! *I love her!*

"Alex, supper is ready."

A voice rises up through the fog, up the stairs to my maddened ears. I speak. I croak. I gasp, in a strangulated whisper that speaks of the inner depravity of a crippled soul, "Okay, I'll be down in a second."

Dear God and gentle reader, forgive me. I must go down and join them and pretend to be their son. Shameful pretense! How gracious is young Alex, they will say. He is a model lad! The paragon of animals! And yet beneath the flesh and bones that they have created, beneath the green sports shirt with small red stripes, beneath the white painter's pants, beneath the sneakers, there lives . . . O God! O God! I am Godzilla in a polo shirt. I am Kong, shot and bleeding, the biplanes buzzing around me. They rip at my flesh. They hurt me, Mother! Stop them! Stop them! Mother, I am dying! I clutch at the TV aerial on the roof. This is the end. I spit blood! The Red Death has me in its power. I love her, Mother! I love Amy Hart! Please, God, make her notice me! Let her see me in Spanish class! In Honors English! Amy, I stand before you, stripped of pride. O God, shoot me dead. I am weak with pain.

I love Amy Hart!

"Alex, this is the last time!"

My poor mother again. O maternal creature cursed with crooked offspring! Had I been shot in the womb with a bazooka, all would be right. But no, God, I live! I live! Amy!

7:10 P.M. Another dinner at the Swinburne mausoleum and investment management center. My father sits with a calculator, studying a pamphlet from the bank. He has a small gray beard, glasses. My mother sips her coffee. She is also reading a pamphlet.

"City Federal is giving eleven nine," she says. "But that's only on the ninety-day."

"Doesn't Carteret have one for fourteen nine?"

"On a fixed rate?"

"I think so. But there's a twenty-thousand-dollar minimum."

My mother looks at my untouched plate.

"Alex, it's growing."

O reader, they mean well I am sure, but even when I attempt to share an experience with them (watching TV!), it just consumes me with contempt. I listen in misery as they prepare for the evening's viewing.

"Who's on *Merv?* Is there anyone good on *Merv?*"

"I don't know," says my father.

"You've got the *Guide.*"

"This is last week's."

"Where's the new one?"

"I thought it was in the bedroom."

"Don't tell me you threw it out again?"

"I didn't throw anything out."

"Now I'll have to go look in the garbage again."

"They *took* the garbage this morning."

O Amy, save me from mediocrity!

Both my brothers were disappointments to my parents. They never did well in school. There was trouble with the police; there were drugs; there were calls from the school principal. And then there was charming Alex who never did anything to embarrass his grateful parents. Even my brothers liked me. And what good, dear reader, has it done me? I live in a dream world. I hide in books; I hide behind my grades. What a dark lie I live!

"Alex, it's still growing."

"All right."

"Are you going anywhere special with Michael tonight?" asks my mother.

"No."

"You ought to do *something* for your birthday."

"I'm going to write in the journal you bought me."

"Oh, that sounds nice."

10:00 P.M. I am calmer now. The weight of homework has dulled the edge of my madness. (So you see, there *is* some purpose to algebra.) Reader, I must tell you the whole story. But how can I when my voice chokes with passion? Let me describe her to you. You, of all people, must understand that which lies beyond logic. Passion is a blind, wild thing. It destroys everything in its path.

O reader, I should be stronger than this. I am an A student. I am on the distinguished Honor Roll. I receive awards for my scholarly achievements. But look at me! I am the unhappiest man on earth. "Look at him!" they say (my enemies, legions of them). "He's got everything!"

Yes, poor Alex Icicle sits by the window in the back of Honors English, smelling of B.O. and chicken soup, and writes in his notebook. Yes, he gets an A on his pronoun quiz. He never raises his voice. He is well mannered. Half-hidden in the shadows in the back of the room, he broods in icy coldness, chained to his cynicism, shackled to his bitterness.

But one day, dear God, he's going to explode! He's going to rip the chains from their massy bolts and rise — the demon, the behemoth — and with dead fingers on arms thirty feet long he will reach to the front of the classroom and grab . . . Amy Hart! The girls will scream; the air will darken. With octopus tentacles, boiling blood, and a dripping V-shaped mouth he will ravage Amy Hart on the classroom floor. Unspeakable! Gentle reader, stop reading now, I pray you. Only those sick of heart need follow from here.

Let me describe her to you. The body is a tall one for an eighth-grader. The hair is straight and short and light brown. Behold, she wears a shirt of antique design, white with a lace collar. She wears jeans that say Prime Cut on the back pocket, and she wears extravagantly striped socks! And Indian moccasins! They are white moccasins with a design in beads stitched upon them. O Amy, dear Amy, dear exalted Amy, I would throw my mother into a pool of sharks if I could kiss one of those white Indian moccasins! (I am sorry, Mother; I apologize to you, but I am mad.) But her shoes, dear reader! You must *see* those white moccasins. And the socks! White woolen socks with cranberry stripes! Each stripe is two inches wide. Her arms are perfect goddess arms in her short-sleeved, antique white shirt. Note how they exquisitely fill the sleeves: golden arms that speak of health, summer and sunshine. My own arms are death-white poles; I have the thinnest arms that have ever been seen on someone who wasn't dead. O God, I *am* dead, tongue dry with corpse dust, formaldehyde in my veins, cold and sick with the moon. I must fashion it into a poem. A death poem! A torment poem! Knell! Knell! The dolorous funeral bell! Ho! for a rhyme!

> *He bears the love of a goddess*
> *deep inside him*
> *growing black*
> *in the darkness*
> *of his heart:*
> *A broken pump*
> *sick with the moon*
> *and bursting with cancer.*

Most excellent! I am collecting all my verse in a volume to be entitled *I Hate Myself: The Suicide Poems of Alexander Preston Sturges Swinburne as Told to Amy Hart Before He Shot Himself Because of Her.* Or maybe *The Human Scum: An Autobiography in Verse.* Or *The Unspeakable Burden of My Desire,* with a cover so obscene that I tremble to think of it. All dedicated to Amy Hart. I dedicate my life to Amy Hart.

O Amy, Amy, I write furiously by flashlight so my parents won't see the light beneath the door.

One day I know I will be discovered. They will smash down the door with fire axes and catch me, horrified and guilty, as I write these words. Flames will leap from my bedsheets! "There!" I will shout, pointing to this wretched journal. "It is the beating of her hideous Hart!" The walls will fall in hellish cinders. The roof will crumble. And a scream will arise from the conflagration like the great crying of a million tortured souls.

Her face! Gentle reader, how can I describe the face upon which I have so meditated? She wears braces. Go ahead, laugh! Laugh at me! Good, I revel in your hate. The more you despise me, the more I know I have succeeded. For I am to be despised and hated as the foulest, most abject creature on earth. I would compare myself to an earthworm but I am far lower. Garden slug! Sick creature of the dead night. Step on me, smash me with a brick, throw me down the toilet, do *anything*, but you must love *her*, gentle reader! For every increment in your loathing of my toadlike presence, you must love her more. You must see her in your mind. The face! The face! Yes, there are braces, but they only enhance the beauty. The complexion is smooth. There are no ravages of adolescence here. Such things do not happen to a goddess. And the brown eyes, reader! The smile! The stately neck, the queenlike carriage! Have you forgotten to observe the tiny silver chain around her neck?

You must see that or you have seen nothing. And the long, sensitive fingers?

She is grace. She is perfection. She rarely speaks in class but when she does all strain forward to hear. The teacher (a withered crone) smiles when Amy speaks. The class sighs at the incandescence of her voice. We are awed that she has consented to break the rarefied vault of her silence to speak to us. A goddess walks the halls of Edison Junior High School! I swear it is true! History will bear me out. She *is* beautiful, sweet reader. And she is nearly as intelligent as I am. I say *nearly* for honesty forces me to confess that there is no one in the school as intelligent as I. But my mind is twisted. Her mind is straight. Where she has used her remarkable powers for good and beauty, I have used mine for sickness and evil. Dear reader, I am anguished and solitary, but I love her. Every minute every pulse of my self-hating heart says *Amy! Amy! Amy!* I draw her name in the air. In typing class I pretend to press the keys of her soft, beautiful name. O wondrous Amy!

But there is something you must know. I look out at this soft May night and I am filled with pain. It is May 30, which as you only too clearly know is my pitiful birthday. I bring it up not to wring from you cheap sentiment, but so you can understand that there are only nineteen days of school remaining. And (I must say it) the unutterable truth is that Amy Hart is moving to California. Her father, I think, is being transferred. A minute does not pass that I do not think of it. If she is absent now for even a day of class, I feel the coming void as nothing but pain.

Time, time, time. It is my greatest enemy. I have barely spoken five sentences to her this year (and those in a haze of self-consciousness). Dear God, let me talk to her before she goes. Let me tell her what I feel. This passion will not, cannot, come again. I am miserable. I lie in bed tonight by this dim flashlight. This is my birthday; dear God, how can she move away? How can you play this monstrous, horrible joke on me? But I will talk to her; it is the one thing I swear I will do. I will tell her. She will laugh, I know. All the world will laugh. But beautiful Amy, I love you; I love you; I love you beyond measure and reason. I hardly know you, Amy, but I swear that the love I feel is like nothing that has ever happened to me before. I cannot explain it.

My flashlight has died. I put on the overhead lamp.

"Alex! It's past midnight! Shut that light off or I'm coming up."

It is my father; dear God, I have so much more to say. But I must shut the light off now. My father yells at me. Dear reader, stay with me. I beg you. Wish me a happy birthday.

2

_____

1:15 P.M. Amy. Amy. Amy. How I chortle, dear reader! I am positively overflowing with excellent news! About what subject? you modestly inquire. I hum, I whistle . . . it's about nothing important . . . only about a goddess on earth and how I'm going to meet her. That's all. Nothing _really_ important, is it? Shall we talk about other things? Shall I tell you about lunch in the school cafeteria today? Shall I tell you about the weather we've been having this late May? What's this? You wish to know about — whom? I didn't catch the name. Amelia? Amanda? Hurt? Hort? Oh! _Amy_ . . . what was it again? Oh yes, _Hart._ That's it. Does _she_ go to Edison? I never knew . . . What? She's in _three_ of my classes? Why, I never even noticed. Imagine that. Right under my nose. Ha! Ha! You must excuse my sportiveness, affectionate reader (and only friend), but I am in high spirits this afternoon as I sit in the rear of study hall — a dark, masked figure wearing a Spanish cloak and black felt boots. Yes, the sound of poisonous laughter (which my enemies have often referred to as both "singular" and *"outré"*) wells up from the cavernous folds of my dusty cloak. I snort. I rattle. But let me tell you in exquisite detail, curious reader. Let me madden you and torture you with the agonizing slowness of my exposition. Yes, you must suffer. As I have suffered the horrors of the eternally damned, so you, too, must suffer. Just remember, however, that your suffering is giving me pleasure.

How shall I begin this Byzantine web of events? Perhaps I shall begin in gym class. Yes, that would be a good place, and if you follow very carefully, you may observe Amy Hart in a state of partial undress. Yes, my suddenly inflamed and heavy-breathing reader, a careful study of these next few pages will reveal all that the sick, vile, obsessive student desires to satisfy his most unwholesome appetites.

Yes, follow me as I take you lower, lower, and lower still into the cesspool of madness and desire. She's Snow White, all right, but the dwarves have lost their innocence, and we stand now (you and I) leaning against the cottage door (some might even say *blocking* the cottage door, but I wouldn't say that, would you?), wiping our lips and blinking the fire from our hot eyes. "But where will I sleep?" says Snow White. We snort and we look and we lick our chops and, stop me, reader, stop me from debasing Amy again. Amy, forgive me! But I rush my sordid story. To gym!

Morning broke sweetly over the little athletic playing field behind the small brick schoolhouse. A group of students played a spirited game of baseball, and all seemed to revel in the wholesomeness of the fine spring morning. Then the sky darkened. A great rumbling was heard. Small animals fled in terror. "It's Alex!" someone yelled. "Alex is coming!" White figures in gym suits ran, aghast. The air grew strangely still. Then the side of the building began to rip from its foundation. A monster in a blue gym suit crashed into the open air. It was as tall as a house and horrible beyond words: warted, sweating, deformed, with a bison face and huge oozing tentacles.

Yes, dear reader, I was ready for gym. My uniform had not been washed since Christmas. The blue shorts bloomed around my legs like scarecrow pants on a tomato stick. I was a frightful apparition.

I stood with Michael in left field. Michael is a far more normal eighth-grader than myself. He is small, hunched, shrunken, gnomelike, bitter.

He is what the world laughably calls my best friend. But Michael and I stood and talked as cynical men of the world. We traded answers on quizzes since we had the same teachers for history and biology, although during different periods. (Keep your eyes open for the nude scene, dear smut-hound reader.)

15

"Answer for an answer," he said.

"All right, all right. The four different kinds of nucleotides in DNA?"

"Too easy. Too easy. Adenine, guanine, thymine, and cy-to-sine, baby."

"Answer for an answer."

"The Big Four at Versailles?" asked Michael.

"And you called mine easy?"

"Who are they, hotshot?"

"Wilson, Clemenceau, Lloyd George, and Orlando, *baaaa*by."

"Answer for an answer? How about a little challenge this time?"

"Spatial configuration of the DNA molecule?"

"Oh, too easy. Double helix, *baaaa*by. The old D.H."

"Hit me with an answer, bro."

"Nineteenth Amendment — year? purpose? and significant David Bowie song?"

"1920. Gave women the franchise. 'Suffragette City,' *baaaa*by!"

"Wham-bam-thank-you-ma'am!"

At these words, reader, a great hush fell over the land. The sun seemed to break through its perpetual screen of darkness, and there fell to earth an almost preternatural illumination. Did my ears perceive the humming of a thousand twangling instruments, or was it only a band saw from the woodshop? Was the air suddenly golden sparkle, diamond rain, pricked with the music of a fairy celesta, or was it only a speck of pollen in my eye?

From out of the ripped wall where Alex the beast had trampled came the courtly masque of eighth-grade girls in glowing white gym suits. One had to shield one's eyes to endure the heart-rushing beauty of it. O pale young women, who make us believe once again in the perfectibility of mankind! (O loathsome, reptilian Alex, who makes us throw in the towel for humanity!)

And there, did you see her? At the front of the line, of course, in the butter sun, with short skirt and golden thigh, with straight hair tossing back in the breeze over a proud, athletic neck: it is Amy Hart! And I stood *exposed* in the field, fifty feet from her. Please, God, let her not look at me! I turn away, hide my scarred face, my skeletal legs, my stinking gym suit. I am naked. I am insect-face, lobster-eyes, clutching claws, O Amy! Throw me in boiling water and slam the lid on the pot. Then weld it shut and drop it in the forgiving sea.

I watched her when she had moved farther away. I watched wonderstruck, and as always I wanted to understand her. What went on inside her head? That's what I longed to know. I wanted to walk home from school with her. I wanted to be with her on a Saturday night. I wanted to stand in line with her at the movies. Just hear her voice.

And I confess it, I've called her house many times. (When I didn't actually call, I dialed the number with the phone still on its cradle.) But sometimes I let it ring once. Just once. It is the secret code I offer to Amy. Please, let her hear it and understand; I am too shy to speak. Sometimes I call late at night and her father answers the phone. "Yello," he says. "Goodbye," I answer.

Amy, why do you never answer the phone? What are you doing? Are you lying on a canopied bed of flowers, surrounded by adoring elves? Do the squirrels bring you bonbons? Does a tiny bird alight on your finger? Were I that bird, to touch your finger! But one touch of my pestilent lips and your hand would shrivel to a warped stump, your perfect skin would peel back and erupt in boils, your eyes would break like egg yolks and the pus would ooze over my lizard hands, balm to the tortured, ointment to the horrible, salve to the bestial! O God, Amy, angels, forgive me. I must speak it! Michael, if I can't tell you then I can tell no one. Confide, Alex!

"What do you think of Amy Hart?" I said, looking abstractedly in her direction.

Michael squinted at the girls playing lacrosse.

"I wouldn't throw her out of bed," he said.

We both glanced at her.

"But she's a snob," he continued.

"Really? Why do you say that?"

18

"I was friends with her a couple of years ago," said Michael. He kicked the grass. "Believe it or not, I had a social life until I met you."

"Why do you say she's a snob?"

"I don't know. She's always seemed kind of untouchable to me. Anyway, that's what Leslie Shapiro says. And they're best friends. Or they used to be. You know that Hart is moving, don't you?"

"I heard something about that."

(Patience, my soul.)

"Yeah, they're moving to California. Anyway, Leslie says she's unbelievably conceited."

My mind was churning. This was all new to me, new scraps of information clutched at with greedy hands and dragged back to the beast's lair. "A snob!" he had said. And "unbelievably conceited." But I have seen her in class; I have observed her carefully; I have listened to every phrase she has uttered. It cannot be true! I will not believe it is true! For me she is the perfect woman. She is my goddess, my muse. Without her there is nothing of value to me in the world. School means nothing to me. I am blind to music, to art, to nature, to everything, if she is not part of it. There is no world without Amy Hart; she is the definition of everything I am, everything I aspire to be. Without her, gentle reader, I have no reason to wake up in the morning.

19

I drive my bicycle past her house hoping to see her. (She lives on Tamaques Way, only a few blocks from my desolate island.) I soar past her peaceful home on the dark, quivering steed of my black desire, and never, *never* have I seen her. But I note the house. There is the doorknob that she touches each day. There is the sidewalk she walks upon.

I often pass by at night to see the house illuminated and warm, refuge to the hurt, birthplace of beauty, incubator of perfection — intelligence, straight brown hair, Prime Cut jeans, and tiny silver chain. And did you remember her striped socks, forgetful reader? Those you must never overlook! Cranberry stripes two inches wide. And the Indian moccasins! Don't tell me you've forgotten them? They are part of my life. I walk by a shoe store, see them in the window, and my poor heart beats faster. Yes, I know that you mock me, impatient reader; you mock me with every fiber of your being. "What does he see in this girl?" you ask. "Why is he so obsessed with her?" I cannot explain it. I cannot get her out of my mind. Do you think I wanted all this pain? I didn't seek this madness.

Of course, I had *seen* her before. We'd even gone to the same elementary school. But that first painful moment of awareness came when I saw her standing outside the cafeteria last October. It was sunny. Michael and I were, as usual, deep in bitter conversation. Amy stood beneath a tree, talking to Leslie Shapiro. She wore her powder-blue ski sweater and her Prime Cut jeans. The sun gently illuminated her face. I seemed to be falling into a dream. I saw her straight brown hair, the sureness of her chin, the modesty of her nose: a kind of elegant demeanor. I was struck by her beauty. But this was a beauty that went beyond the merely physical. Her radiant face seemed to me only a window on the depth within.

Put yourself in my eyes! Take all the images you find most beautiful in the world and distill them into one face. Take all the radiance and loveliness you have seen, felt, or dreamed of, and you will begin to feel the fire of Amy Hart. I worship her. I confess it. I am beyond shame.

And the lies of Leslie Shapiro? "She is a snob." "She is unbelievably conceited." You may believe them if you wish, but let me color your worthy judgment with a brief description of Leslie Shapiro. Gentle reader, I bear the wretched slut no ill will, but I must tell you about her. First, though, I must own up to the most horribly pathetic aspect of my story: Leslie Shapiro likes me. She may even be in love with me. Reader, reader, hateful reader, she asked me to a dance in December at the temple youth group, and *I refused.* I dared to refuse an overture of friendship, possibly of love. It was the first I had ever been offered, and I refused. I said I was busy. Miserable self! (If Amy is the essence of all that is virtuous and beautiful, I am the essence of all that is self-serving and mean-spirited.)

Let me give you the story. Leslie Shapiro is in my class. She is what is compassionately called a "plain" girl. She has dark hair and a nose that is somewhat too big. (Leslie, I am sorry for this description, but I cannot stop. It is not Alex who destroys you. It is his madness.) Her features have something witchlike about them. She smiles at me in the hall. She sometimes stands by my locker. She seems to find me in the lunch line. God help me, but I dread her. I avoid her with calculation. It is not that she is particularly unpleasant, but (my motive is piteous — stab me in the eye with a barbeque skewer) I am afraid that Amy Hart will see us together and think that I have a girlfriend. I want to make sure that Amy knows I'm free from "entangling alliances." As I write these words I cover my face in shame. How can a human being sink as low as I have?

Poor Leslie, I do not ask for your forgiveness or for your compassion. I dare imagine that Amy Hart might want to love me. The smallest of men has the most limitless of dreams!

Amy Hart stood with her hand on her hip watching the lacrosse ball.

"Answer for an answer?"

"What?"

"Why are you suddenly so interested in Amy Hart, anyway?" said Michael.

"I don't know."

He smiled broadly.

"Well, well. Don't tell me Mr. I-Don't-Associate-with-People-Who-Associate-with-Girls has finally been smitten?"

"Shut up. Answer for an answer. Explain the difference between messenger and transfer RNA and summarize how messenger RNA acts as a template for the synthesis of polypeptide chains."

"So it's Amy Hart, huh?"

I couldn't help laughing, I didn't know what to think. How I longed to tell him!

"You know, Leslie Shapiro's giving a surprise party for her Friday night. In fact, she asked me if you wanted to go. I said I didn't think so."

"Yeah?"

"If you want to go, I'll tell her. You *know* Leslie's got the hots for you."

The sun was warm on the field.

"Are you going?"

"Yeah," he said. "Why don't you show up?" He twisted his face. "Or isn't it *educational?*"

The blood was pounding in my head. My throat was dry.

"So it's Amy Hart." He chuckled. "Wait till I tell Leslie."

"Don't, Michael."

"Oh, he's worried now, is he?"

I looked at him.

"Don't worry, bro," he said.

The whistle was blown to go inside. I deliberately slowed my pace so Amy would go through the door far ahead of me.

"Do you want me to tell Leslie you're coming?" he asked.

My legs were shaking. Shadows flashed before me.

"Yes."

O reader, I fell into swooning disorientation. The locker room was a dreamlike crazy house of slamming doors and steaming showers. The floor tilted beneath my feet . . . Friday night! For once I would not be alone with my books: my *Hamlet*, my Poe. Instead I would be at a party in honor of Amy Hart! I would be there! I would not imagine it; I would not ride by on my bicycle, but I, monster among the living, Nosferatu among the young and innocent, would be *with* her. Dressed as an ordinary human. I could finally watch her away from school. I could hear what she said. Every wondrous detail! Perhaps let her know, in small ways, how I cared. O Amy, no human on earth cares for you the way I do. I long to tell you this.

The study-hall bell just rang.

Jubilation! Amy, I love you!

3

9:00 **P.M.** Patient reader, I have much to report. (How are you, my silent friend?) I have much to tell you, and I have hungered for a moment of solitude to express all these strange emotions.

I passed the afternoon at Michael's house with another "friend," Jim Keating. We three sat up in Michael's tiny, dark bedroom. The walls are painted purple. In the manner typical of my embarrassing peers there are posters all around. One says LIFE IS A GAS AT $1.15 9/10. Another says LET'S TWIST AGAIN, with a picture of a marijuana cigarette. (Reader, I may be wretched but am I any worse than the times I live in?)

I sat on Michael's bed reading *Mad* magazine, half listening to the conversation. Michael, hunched over his desk lamp, was soldering a patch cord. Jim Keating sat on a speaker listening to Michael's rare monaural pressing of *Sergeant Pepper*. I say I was reading, but my mind was far away. It was, of course, with Amy.

"Did you hear that Alex is in love?" said Michael.

I kept my eyes on the magazine. ("The Lighter Side of: Obsession")

"Who with?" Keating asked me.

"He's crazy," I said.

I never liked Keating much. He was a normal-looking fourteen-year-old, about eight feet tall, with horrible acne that covered every square inch of his flesh. There was acne on top of acne. He was encrusted with the loathsome stuff, like some ghastly mummy. And yet (strangeness of the human condition) he was one of the most popular boys in school. I attributed this (with my keen analytical powers) to his height, his sturdiness, the freak of his maturing faster than the rest of us.

Thoughtful reader, how often have I contemplated this painful phenomenon. I've watched the "successes" as they move down the hall with their lustful arms draped around some mindless, though inevitably beautiful, woman. Is it fair that such spoils should fall their way? They joke with the teachers as though they were adults; they're stars in athletics; they're photographed at the prom. Oh, insufferable jealousy of the runts! Because I am thin and small they assume that I have a child's mind. If only they could see! I love with a passion that dwarfs their own!

"This boy," said Michael, "this here boy is, what you call, in love."

"Do *you* know who?" asked Keating.

"Yup," said Michael. The smoke from the soldering gun rose around his head.

"Who is it?"

"Ask him."

"I'd rather not talk about it," I said. "I'm reading."

"Yes," said Michael acidly. "Love isn't *educational*, we all know that."

"This is interesting," said Keating. "Would you tell me if I guessed right?"

"The subject doesn't interest me."

"It's Leslie Shapiro, isn't it? Just tell me yes or no."

"The subject doesn't interest me."

"Yes or no."

"No."

"I saw you two walking down the hall the other day."

(Dear God, did Amy see it as well?)

"It's not Leslie Shapiro," I said, rolling the name across my tongue with disgust. "I do have some taste."

Keating found a piece of paper and a pen. "I'm going to figure this out. Is she in our class?"

"This is stupid."

"*Is* she?"

"Yes!"

I clutched the magazine for strength.

"Is she blond?"

"No."

"Brunette?"

"Yes."

He was writing down names on his pad. He would pause, sink into the silence of his mummified, acned brain, then write some more.

"And you'll tell me if I guess it?"

"I'll let you make one guess."

Michael gave me a death-grin. Curse his gnomelike face!

"Is she very good-looking, moderately good-looking, or a dog?"

Horrified reader, what could I say?

"I don't know what your scale is."

Michael laughed. "Leslie Shapiro is a dog."

"A double-bagger," said Keating. "You need a bag over her head *and* a bag over yours."

"I don't know," I said.

"She's moderately good-looking," said Michael.

(Amy Hart is beautiful! I could show you a thousand photographs, and you would pick her out at once. There would be no need to continue. You would stop and say, "This is she.")

"All right, is she on this list?" said Keating. He tossed the pad to me.

I held the odious document in trembling hands. The fool had scrawled a pathetic list of candidates:

1. *Ilene Gelbein*
2. *Laurie Rosen*
3. *Olivia Laffey*
4. *Vicki Milne*
5. *Emily Mercer*
6. *Andrea Gilpen*
7. *Marybeth English*
8. *Yvonne Weeks*
9. *Heather Karl*
10. *Amy Hart*
11. *Roberta Rusch*
12. *Toby Palmer*

My discriminating reader, have you ever seen such a miserable list of slatterns and whores, saved only by one brief, radiant star: three syllables of unparalleled purity. The other names are nothing. They are faces in any junior high school in any town in the world. But Amy shines forth as solitary and perfect.

"Is she on the list?"

"Yes."

He got up and took the pad. (A curse on fourteen-year-olds who look like they're in their twenties. I hate him *intensely!*)

The creature leaned against the mirror. He held the pen before him to eliminate names.

"Does she have big tits?"

(I am sorry, sensitive reader, but I must report what was said.)

"Moderate."

Michael snorted bitterly. "Pirate's delight," he said.

"Oh," said Keating. "Sunken chest."

(Reader, please remember her great beauty; see again her tiny silver chain, her majestical face, the brown hair, the stripes! Have you forgotten to visualize the white socks with the two-inch cranberry stripes?)

"Good legs?"

"Moderate," I said.

(What could I say? Could I mention the countless times I had walked behind her on the stairs and observed the beauty of her legs, the arch and muscle, the form and line?)

"Good ass?"

"I don't know."

"I mean, is she a girl with heavy-duty shock absorbers?"

Both he and Michael laughed riotously at this.

"Is she bright?"

"Very."

He crossed a few names off the list.

"How about her personality? Is she outgoing? Is she quiet?"

Michael looked up from his soldering.

"She's a snob," he said.

Keating put down the pad. "Oh, then it's Amy Hart." He looked toward me.

"Is that your guess?" I said.

"Yes. Is it Amy Hart?"

"No."

Michael glared at me with hatred. And hatred I deserved, for lying. But, compassionate reader, I showed them a goddess, and they asked me if she had big tits.

"Then I don't know who it is," said Keating. He put down the pen on the dresser. "But if it is Amy Hart you might as well forget it. She's been throwing herself on Alex Lewis all year. And he doesn't even like her that much. He said she's a snob. He said she's got an ego bigger than a goddamn house."

It was a difficult and lonely journey from Michael's house back to my own. His corrosive laughter mocked me. I passed through black forests and quaint villages. Cities drifted about me, haunted by the sad ghosts of wasted lives. "Amy!" they called in woeful tones from the shadows. They held out their hands beseechingly, as if I could impart some dread secret to end their misery. "Amy!" I heard them in the dark shipyards where the water lapped on the tarred poles; I heard them in the dismal alleys. Soon I had walked the four blocks to my house. I fell among those eating supper.

"Does she have big tits?" asked my father.

"What?"

"I said these cherries have big pits."

He placed one in the ashtray. I looked at him carefully. He had short gray hair, a modest gray beard, and gentle eyes. I observed my mother as well. She was large, slightly weary-looking, but had a tenderness that tempered with sensitivity and humor.

I pitied them, dear reader. I pitied them that they were cursed with a son like me, who sat locked in miserable silence for a whole meal, aching, aching to tell them all I had endured. But I said nothing. I thought only of Amy. Amy. She'd been "throwing herself" on Alex Lewis all year? Could it be true? And I had never seen it! I, who have made my life's work the study of Amy Hart! I have seen nothing!

But Alex Lewis, gentle reader? Could it be? Do you know him? He, too, was in our class. He was another one like Keating, physically swollen beyond his years. And, God help me, he was handsome. He was everything I was not. Even a poor, limping toad can recognize the strengths of others. He is large, stocky, powerful. He has the shadow of a beard. Fourteen, and he can grow a beard! He sits in my study hall: silent, slow, deliberate, a little bit oafish. I sometimes even help him with his homework. God, the man is a dullard! The goddess is throwing herself on a dullard! Can the world be so unjust? How can God be so unfair? (I would be hurt by her loving *anyone* else — but for the most beautiful to love the most mediocre?)

10:00 P.M. I must talk to her. I must tell her something of what I feel, and I resolve tonight that whatever the consequences I will tell her. She will laugh. She will giggle over it with Alex Lewis, tell her whole lunch table. But I will speak with her. Oh, I feel weak. Sometimes I feel I am drifting into real madness. I must get hold of myself. Let me plan my dark course of action.

First, I will deliberately ingratiate myself with Alex Lewis. We were good friends once. In sixth grade I recall noticing that not only were our first names the same, but our birthdays were the same as well. We bought small metal calendars, disks the size of a half dollar, and called ourselves the "calendar brothers." I will mention all this to him again! Starting tomorrow in study hall I will begin the slow process of gaining his confidence. I will pump him on the subject of Amy Hart. I will learn his secret — what makes him attractive to her. I do not have much time. School is ending so quickly. Just three weeks and then it is exam schedule.

But there are two new developments I see as significant.

This Wednesday and Thursday is the biology field trip. The classes travel by bus to some weed-strewn campsite in north Jersey and there we collect mud. But I am going. And Michael is going. And Jim Keating is going. And the beautiful Amy Hart is going! She and I will be alone! Alone! There *have* been stories, saucy reader, I am sure you know. Yes, the biology field trip is positively legendary in its stories of sexual debauchery and violent diarrhea. Just the walls of rustic cabins, my sick, hopeful reader, just small cabin walls separate the men from the women. And there are no parents! There are simply a few meager chaperones. But who is to prevent a young beast from standing in the darkness and peering through the window of her cabin as she undresses? (I am sick. Forgive me, Amy. But I am driven. I must talk to you before I do something really mad. I want to call your home again, but I dare not. The police are waiting, I know.)

And then there is the party on Friday night! This will be a week crammed with incident! Amy! I know I will have my chance to speak to you at last. Please listen, Amy. I do exist. (I love you!) God, give me time at the party. I must tell her. And I will learn from Alex Lewis the secrets of winning her heart. Sometimes, sometimes, enchanted reader, the lonely frog-prince *can* win the hand of the princess. It does happen; I know it does. It must.

It is late. I write now by flashlight again. I dream, dear reader, of a knock on the door. I look up and it is Amy. Her lips are melting soft now. Soft.

3:01 A.M. I awaken from a feverish dream: Amy Hart was sitting on a park bench. She turned to the side and for one second I could see her bra strap. God, I am sick.

There is a ghastly wet stain across the top sheet. I sicken myself. If I had actually made love to her in my dream, perhaps I wouldn't mind. But to have become so overwrought at the sight of a bra strap? I have failed even in my dreams.

Reader, I am sick of your understanding and patience. You do not fool me with your knowing smile. You see everything, don't you? You know all the answers, don't you? Well, did you notice anything about that list of girls' names a few pages back? You didn't? I suppose it never occurred to your supremely gifted mind that the list might have some significance? Still not with me? Then, going down the list, read the first letter of each girl's name. Now, isn't that interesting? Yes, it was there the whole time. And you never saw it. And just think how many other secrets are hidden within this manuscript that I will *never* tell you about.

P.S. Amy, forgive me.

4

8:40 A.M. I must kill Alex Lewis.

(I apologize for my bitterness of last night. The nights are difficult on my island; the air is full of demons. I hope you will accept my apology, dear reader. Think of me as a sick friend whom you are obliged to visit in the mental institution. You sit by my bedside, in terrified sympathy, while I weave in the air spells of gossamer lunacy.)

Alex Lewis must die, but the method must be inspired. I could dismember him in the cellar and plaster him in the walls, but there would always be the chance that a hideous black cat would be walled in with him, screeching, red-mouthed, at the moment of my triumph. (It *has* happened.) No, my method must be more foolproof and less literary.

I write these murderous notes in biology. The teacher is going over the principles of DNA replication because everyone in the class (except one) failed yesterday's test. (Need I tell you who that wretched one was? The class has always hated me; this has only intensified their loathing.) But, my conspiratorial reader, this pointless review session has given me a moment to speak to you. It will be difficult to speak to you in study hall anymore, because I must spend my time talking to Alex Lewis. The fat dolt! Pathetic rival for her affections! What worth is an opponent who is so intellectually puny? Professor Moriarty *needed* to fight Sherlock Holmes; anyone else was a waste of his talents. But I have no Holmes to battle. I have only the fumbling Watson.

Do I seriously contemplate murder, my friend? I think not. I dare not actually hurt anyone. Hurt implies power over others, and I have no power over anyone. Nor do I want it. But it is a lively morning. My classmates sit in forlorn misery. Imagine! They are upset over a test! They see a red-marked ditto as a measure of their self-worth! Have you ever seen anything so ridiculous? What would they do had they the motive and the cue for passion that I have? They would drown the lab tables with tears! For what's DNA to them or they to DNA that they should weep for it? Amy! Amy!

I tap my pen on the lab table and see where a tortured mind has carved a name deep into the surface. Let us look a little closer. Observe, it is a woman's name! How exceedingly charming.

Why, these junior high students actually believe they're in love! Oh, isn't that rich!

12:35 P.M. Lunch. Leslie Shapiro has just left my table. On "B" days she and I eat together. (I keep changing my seat but she still finds me.)

I was sitting alone in the far corner when she swooped energetically upon me, her tray laden with enough food for three people.

"Why do you wear your top button buttoned?" she demanded.

"I like it that way."

"*No*body wears their top button buttoned."

"I like it."

"It makes me so hot. God, I feel like I'm strangulating just looking at it."

"Sorry."

"Only wimps button their top button."

"Did you sit here to insult me?"

"Oh!" she said. "Today it's going to be Mr. Leave-Me-Alone-I'm-Contemplating-the-Meaning-of-Life."

"Sorry."

"You're in school, Alex. This *is* life! There are people around here! You're supposed to *talk* to people."

"I think you probably do enough talking for both of us."

"I have to! Don't I? If I waited for you, God knows where I'd be. You know what I'm waiting for?"

I sighed. "Leslie, why do you always ask me questions like that? You always say 'Guess what?' or 'Do you know what happened today?' How am I supposed to answer that?"

"But do you *know* what I'm waiting for? Do you know what I'm really waiting for?"

I shook my head. "What?"

"I'm waiting for the day that *you* ask me out. That you ask me anything! That you *initiate* any human activity. Really! If Mike and I didn't club you over the head, I think you'd spend your entire life in your room."

"Stop."

She sang to the tune of "In My Room."

> *There's a world where I can go*
> *And tell my secrets to,*
> *In my womb,*
> *In my womb.*

"Very funny."

"It's true!"

She buttered a roll vigorously.

"Alex, I'm waiting for the day that you say, 'Leslie, do you want to go to the movies tonight?' *Not* like Mike and I are dragging you — and you're *reluctantly* coming along. Do you think I'll ever see that day?"

"I don't like going to the movies."

"*I* know. You can't stand crowds."

"I can't."

"You can't stand crowds because crowds are *life*. God forbid anybody touches you or *sneezes* on you. I think you wash your hands more than any person on the planet."

"And you're the exact opposite! The other day at the Dairy Queen you ate your hamburger right after playing Asteroids. I mean how many greasy hands have touched those buttons? And you didn't even care. You just grabbed your hamburger."

"And I'm still alive, Alexander! I didn't drop dead. Sometimes you have to *touch* things in this world and sometimes you have to get out and *grab* things and *do* things and sometimes you have to ask people out to the movies."

"I don't like going to the movies."

She shrieked in aggravation. "If I didn't like you so much, I'd kill you."

1:30 P.M. Contact made with Alex Lewis! I've moved back to my corner of the room, and I can barely mask my demonic glee! Watch me carefully, Lewis; watch as your "calendar brother" slowly and secretly draws his plans against you. There will be no mistake. And I have not forgotten about murder! No, the thought is heavy in my mind now, the thousand dazzling schemes. Lewis, you are not so hard a bear to bait!

Perhaps a line of SweeTarts down the hallway leading to the incinerator (a hole in the custodian's room covered by a heavy cement disk).

You'll bend down for the last purple SweeTart, and I'll push you in with a broomstick. I'll shove the cement disk shut and throw the switch, laughing maniacally as I hear the sweet flames below sizzling with your fat!

Or perhaps I'll come into the school at night, with a grindstone and a welder's visor, with sparks flying, I'll grind the edge of my locker to razor sharpness. "Oh, Alex!" I shall sweetly call to my rival. "Would you look in my locker a second — I think I left my tuba on the top shelf." He sticks his head within and *slam!* Slice! God! What a tragedy!

Or I'll spread Krazy Glue on his handlebars. He'll roll into traffic and realize with sinking horror that he's out of control. A lumbering flatbed truck filled with steel girders moves down the hill in his direction! Oh, the horror! The tragedy!

And speaking at his funeral, the class valedictorian and best friend the deceased ever had, Mr. Alexander Preston Sturges Swinburne. (A ridiculous name, I know, embarrassed reader, bestowed upon me by a mother with perhaps overly artistic aspirations.) The valedictorian speaks. He intones! There in the front row of the cathedral (Oh, the sobbing) is the broken and bereaved Amy Hart. She weeps bitterly, abandoning herself to the torrent of grief inside her. (Patience, sweet woman! Time and faith, time and faith.) I stand at the towering pulpit in giant carmine robes; I throw my hands up. Tears stream down my cheeks uncontrollably. (I have a bag of onions hidden in the lectern.)

Later, Amy comes to me, her face is a mask of woe. She takes my hand. "It was a wonderful speech, Alex." I clasp her precious, warm hands. (Oh, the touch!) "Time and faith, Amy, time and faith." With my head reverentially bowed I can clearly see her white Indian moccasins. My heart is suddenly seized with desire. I throw myself at her feet and begin kissing her adored moccasins. "Father!" she exclaims. "What are you doing?" I kiss her ankles madly. "Amy, I have always loved you! I know I have taken a vow to devote my life to God, but *you* are God, Amy."

I lift her in my arms and leap to the huge chandelier. I swing over the screaming congregation and break through the stained-glass window into the rain-swept night.

Amy, I watch the object of your affection as he sits and plays with a thumbtack. (The hopeless oaf!) I spoke to him, Amy. I approached him a few minutes after the bell rang, under the pretense of asking to borrow his algebra book. (Oh, most useless of subjects!) Naturally, as men of the world, we sat and talked a few moments. I perched on the windowsill, looking occasionally into the courtyard. He sat at his too-small desk. He wore sandals, a green Ocean Pacific shirt, and cut-offs that seemed to be bursting at the seams.

He had a beat-up pile of books and a tattered blue binder scribbled with the names of repulsive, heavy-metal rock bands (Youth in Asia, Iron Testicles). Curse my singular powers of observation, but I could see that on the spine of the binder was also written *Amy*, retraced a hundred times with a ball-point pen. Detestable lover! How embarrassingly obvious and pedestrian! Can you imagine? He writes her name as if it were a magical incantation!

"You going on the bio field trip tomorrow?" I asked. I yawned. I stretched. I squinted elaborately.

"Are you kidding? Bio! That's all I need. I'm failing earth science now."

"You get to miss two days of school."

"Yeah, I can see doing that."

I laughed mirthlessly. "You know what I was thinking about the other day?" I said. "God, I don't even know if you'll remember this. Remember when we were both in, like, fifth or sixth grade? And we had these dopey little perpetual calendars? These little metal things. Do you remember that? We used to call ourselves the 'calendar brothers.' Do you remember that?"

"No."

"These little green disks?" I gestured feebly.

"I don't remember."

"Oh, well, it's nothing. I mean it just crossed my mind the other day. I remember we called ourselves the 'calendar brothers.' "

"Yeah?" He shook his head.

"Well, your birthday is May thirtieth, isn't it?"

"Yeah," he said. "Is that yours?"

"Sure."

"You've got a good memory."

Oh, how could *you* remember, you corpulent pig! You have newer, fresher memories of Amy Hart and her soft brown hair, which you (fatted manure bucket) have undoubtedly caressed. Why would you dwell in the dead past as I do, when you can touch Amy Hart? When was the last time she allowed you to touch her? When was the last time she "threw herself on you," you running sore?

"Oh, I remember nearly everything," I said. He was looking impatient. I pointed to the name on his binder. "Amy Hart?" I asked.

He nodded, scratching his throat.

"I thought I saw you two together."

"Do you know her?" he asked.

"Well, I know her friend Leslie. I'm good friends with Leslie Shapiro."

"Oh, Leslie-the-Witch." He laughed. He had large teeth. "That's what Amy calls her. Leslie-the-Witch."

"Yeah," I said. "She does sort of look like a witch."

"Amy's moving, you know." He actually looked a little sad.

"I didn't know."

He nodded. "Yeah. She's moving to California on June twenty-fifth."

"The twenty-fifth, huh?"

"Yeah, a Saturday."

(He knew *exactly* what day it was. What did he plan to do the night before, the beast? What last-minute present was he going to thrust upon her?)

"Have you been going with her long?"

"Just this last couple months. On and off."

"Leslie's pretty sad to see her go," I said.

Lewis shrugged his shoulders. "What can you do?"

He certainly wasn't going to admit that *he* was sad. I studied the thickness of his coarse hands. I observed with sinking heart the hairiness of his legs. I observed his snarled sideburns. Muscular oaf! Beach clown! He had short black hair; he looked as if he needed sleep. His face was pale and tight with that premature aging one sees in people who take drugs.

O Amy! You "throw yourself" on him? And will you cry over *him* when you leave? Will you cry to leave your brainless, hairy-legged, dissipated fool? Amy, he will never love you. How can he be the one to tear at your heart as you tear at mine? I love you deeper than any man has loved a woman. But Alex Lewis? Amy! You will become like all the rest. He'll strip you of your magic. O Amy, I want to be like the prince who leads Snow White away on his horse toward the enchanted kingdom. I cry at the end of *Snow White*. I cry for all the hopeless beauty I seek in my life that will never be.

And then I look and see Alex Lewis, sitting fat and contented, playing with a thumbtack. O Amy, Amy, he'll belch as he leads you away on his horse toward the enchanted kingdom. He'll complain about the heat. You'll have an argument about where to go for dinner. His castle will be cold. You'll feel a little sick and discover you have cancer. And you'll have to have a breast removed . . .

O Amy, forgive me for the sickness of my brain!

6:00 P.M. The bell rang, and I drifted through the halls of Edison Junior High School. I listened to the slamming lockers.

"Alex!" came a voice.

Reader, who should accost me but Leslie Shapiro. She flagged me down by my razor-edged locker. She means well, she tries so hard, and I am so wretched to her. But all I saw as she spoke was Amy Hart walking with her arm around the waist of Alex Lewis. Dear God, they walked in a slow, sad, romantic haze. All the hall drifted away except for them. They walked so slowly! Her arm lingered around his waist.

Leslie pulled at my shirttail.

"Mike says you can come to my party on Friday?"

"If it's okay with you."

"Sure! It's great."

She was bouncing up and down to some song inside her head.

"It's a surprise party, though, so don't say anything to anybody."

"Fine."

"Do you know what bus you're on for the field trip tomorrow?"

I fumbled for my books. "No. No. I didn't check."

"The list's over by the history office. C'mon, let's go look."

The hall was just a haze to me. Amy had faded into the crowd.

"Let's go look." She was genuinely excited.

"Okay, okay."

"Amy's going to get there about seven-thirty on Friday. So you've got to be there earlier. You know my address?"

"Michael does."

"Give me a piece of paper; I'll write it down."

I walked next to her like a drugged man. I wondered if I would be on Amy's bus. Perhaps we would be assigned seats next to each other (after all, Swinburne is next to Hart), and she would sit by the window and every time the bus turned left I would *lean* against her. Oh, my brain sickness! And I would have to place my hard-back copy of *Biological Science* on my lap to cover the mountain of my insane desire. (Shoot me in the head, sympathetic reader.)

And you know only too well what the ditto read. There upon the glass, held by two pieces of transparent tape, were the names and bus assignments. Amy headed the list! It made me happy to see her stand above all the others. And my name, misspelled as usual, was lost among the physical failures of Bus Two. Mocking Fate had steered me (hand on my shoulder) directly to the losers' bus. With Leslie Shapiro.

"Good, we can sit together," she said.

I could have cried.

11:00 P.M. I've just finished watching *The List of Adrian Messenger* on television. During my favorite part of the film, Leslie called.

"Should I bring my portable backgammon for the bus?" she asked.

My heart fell. "I don't know how to play."

"I'll teach you."

"I'm terrible at box games, Leslie."

"Good, I like to win."

I made it back to the film. (All this will be important later on, anxious reader. Remember, time and faith. I know you're impatient for the nude scene, for the scene in which I stand outside Amy's cabin and vividly describe the mesmeric radiance of her pajamas, but you must be patient.)

What appeals to me most about *The List of Adrian Messenger* is its brilliant and secret conclusion. (I applaud its cunning!) The murder has been solved; the hounds are baying; the fox hunt is over. Suddenly a voice speaks to us. Can you imagine speaking *directly* to the audience in a work of fiction, gentle reader?) The voice says: "Stop! Hold it! That's the end of the picture . . . but it's not the end of the *mystery!*" As a strange, minor-key melody plays, we watch amazed as the characters of the film remove their masks. They peel back rubber noses and pull out artificial teeth. Look, the gypsy stableman was Frank Sinatra! The stout woman who protested the fox hunt was Burt Lancaster! I am drawn to this scene over and over. How much easier my life would be if I could be a gypsy stableman, a stout woman with a protest placard, some *character*, any character but myself.

Compassionate friend, how I long to be someone else. If only I could look upon the world through the deep protection of an impenetrable mask. My parents continually ask me what I want to be "when I grow up" (ridiculous expression!), and I inevitably respond with "talk-show host," but how much richer to be a mask-maker! How much more satisfying to be the maker of secret monsters. I would sit in my workshop full of magician's cabinets, trick mirrors, skulls with speakers hidden inside, sliding bookcases, hidden staircases, invisible wires: a great fun house where illusions are created. O magic world!

Before me lies my suitcase, in which I must pack the necessary clothing for my two-day trip into the enchanted forest (enchanted with Amy). I must pack my usual garb: tuxedo and tails, gorilla suit, false beard, dark glasses, backpack jet-propulsion unit, opera cape, and appearing cane. In addition, of course, I must bring *Hamlet,* Poe, and Conan Doyle — singing-masters of my soul! Sometimes I believe I am Hamlet reborn. Have you ever noticed that if you rearrange the letters of *Hamlet,* they spell *Alexander Preston Sturges Swinburne?* And have you noticed that if you rearrange the letters of *Ophelia* they spell *Amy Hart?* Very few critics have commented on this fact. Even A. T. Hyram, in his classic *Shakespearean Cryptograms,* fails to observe this obvious reference. But, I suppose, one should never expect too much from a critic whose name is an anagram for a goddess. (Oh, I am in a crafty mood this evening! Somehow I feel that good things are on their way!) Amy, I wish you were here to share this strange happiness with me. How I love you tonight, beautiful girl!

Ah, tired reader, that's the end of the chapter. But it's not the end of the mystery.

5

8:50 A.M.

"Your top button is still buttoned."

I hold my head in misery. The bus sits with its motor running in front of the school. Leslie is beside me.

"Why are you always holding your head in your hands?"

"Because life is so wonderful."

"I think it *is* pretty wonderful," she says.

I moan.

"Really, Alex, what do you have to be so miserable about?"

"I'm miserable because life isn't full of hushed, fervent mystery."

"Do you want to learn backgammon now?"

"No."

"I thought it might cheer you up."

"I *am* cheerful."

"You could have fooled me," she says and taps her finger on the glass.

"I *am* cheerful, Leslie. But the joy I feel is inside me."

"Oh, heavy," she says. "Very heavy. High marks in heaviosity."

"Thank you."

"Now all you have to do is learn to touch a public telephone, and I think you're ready for life."

9:00 A.M. (On the road.)

Do I long to be exposed? Why else would I bring this accursed manuscript with me on the bus (knowing it could be wrested from my hands and read to the whole jeering crowd)? Why else would I be writing now, leaning shoulder to shoulder with Leslie Shapiro? (She doesn't look too bad today.) But I shield my guilty, self-damning words with my left hand as we jostle out of town and the green-tinted light flashes around me. Far ahead sit Michael and Keating. I unfortunately have the seat over the wheel, and my legs are jammed up uncomfortably. Leslie tries to read what I am writing, but I coyly assert, "It's a novel," and this leaves her impressed enough to leave my reverie unbroken. Ha! Dear reader, she does not guess the depths of cruelty that lie within the beast who sits next to her. (*The Beast on the Bus.* Good title.)

My pen bounces unsteadily as we leave town.

The adolescent horrors around me scream with recognition as we pass their streets: Amy Drive, Amy Circle, Amy Way, Amy Crescent. Her bus weaves unsteadily before ours. I try to glimpse her but cannot. There is so much noise in this bus it is difficult to think. The trip is less than ten minutes old, and already they are eating. Behind me I smell loathsome bologna (odor most nauseating to my sensibilities), and someone has sprayed the entire rear of the bus with a can of soda.

Dear reader, is there anything more repulsive than a bus of eighth-graders? I apologize for my generation. I am embarrassed for my whole sickening class. We are the generation that offers nothing but loudness and cruelty. (And I do not exclude myself from this bitter survey. I may be the cruelest of all.) Leslie has insisted that she teach me backgammon! O grasping harpy! O clutching shrike! You see, perceptive reader, her respect for writers was short-lived.

It is probably around 11:00 P.M. I write once again by flashlight. This morning seems a sunlit dream compared to the insults and debasing humiliations of tonight. These cabins have no showers, and I feel layered with grime — physical and spiritual. How I wish I could start my life again. (Or at least take a shower.) I feel imprisoned. I think I must have a fungus on my scalp. I pull horrible-smelling white scales from the roots of my hair. My fingers are greasy with them. The other day I examined one under my microscope. It looked like a lunar crater. How I wish I could pull all this imprisoning, revolting stuff off my head in one motion, just somehow lift this disgusting skullcap of heat and leave my brain cool, tender, and raw. But I write with this massy horror clamped around my brain, and the thoughts inside are even more repulsive than the diseased sheath that cloaks them.

I am on the top of a bunk bed in this flimsy cabin. At least I have a back room in this warehouse of teen-age excrement. Below me sleeps Art Mahy, lost in the slumber of the innocent. I hear him breathing regularly (no accelerated gasping like my own, culminating in unspeakable release). Outside, in the main room, I hear a radio playing softly. Let me tell you what happened. (Brace yourself.)

Leslie, indeed, taught me backgammon on the bus. I told her that box games bored me. She insisted. The only darkly humorous pleasure I received was that I won every game we played. This infuriated her, and I found her anger comforting.

The day passed with an indifferent group of seven; we searched the forest for the various items on our ditto. I was in charge of conifers, and I had to identify pine, spruce, fir, cedar, hemlock, yew, and larch. The afternoon felt like a kind of treasure hunt. There were the usual incidents. Someone fell in the pond. Some boys found an abandoned swimming pool filled with frogs, and they heartlessly pelted the poor creatures with rocks until a chaperone discovered them. I saw the three smirking about it later. (O gentle reader, is there any limit to human cruelty?)

But I stray from my theme, which is and always must be Amy Hart. She was the true treasure hunt. It was an afternoon filled with glimpses of Amy. I would be lost among the giant pines, dazed and alone, then suddenly look ahead to see Amy standing in a pool of sunlight at the foot of the mammoth trees. (This grove had been planted during the Depression, and the mathematical precision of the rows lent an even more enchanted air to the forest.) She stood at the base of the trees, on a bed of pine needles, in soft, honeyed sunlight. She wore blue shorts and bright blue socks. Her shirt was a white sailor's pullover with blue piping. She was my sailor of the forest! My fairy-tale sailor! She wrote with seriousness on the clipboard she held. The bright blue of her outfit shone out among the more subdued hues of the forest. She looked like a colorfully dressed angel who had fallen to earth with a clipboard. Her assignment was to report back about life on earth. How industrious she was at her task. Look at her writing, dear reader! O enchanted sailor, you illuminate my miserable world.

I watched her as if in a dream. Then someone called her, and she flickered into the shadows. (Do I wake or sleep?) These small moments of radiance (Amy stopping to pick a twig out of her sneaker, Amy washing mud from her fingers under the faucet) made the day bearable.

There was a moment when, standing alone in a sunlit field, I smelled the dirt my feet kicked up, I smelled the bramble, the honeysuckle breeze, the secret coolness of the surrounding forest, and it seemed to me timeless and beautiful. I imagined the world before cars and telephone wires. Nature seemed to speak to me of the enormous potential of man. I was sadly moved, gentle reader.

But winds blew through my spellbound sanctuary, and I hurried back to join the rambling, indifferent others, who were planning a softball game. A large bell with a hand rope was sounded dramatically over the little village of lake and field and cabin. We had supper on school tables in a large wooden dining hall, eating roast beef from chipped plates. Then there arrived a perforated cardboard box, steaming with cold, filled with cups of Italian ice. Everyone grabbed greedily for his favorite flavor; I was ready to do the same when I noticed that across the room Amy had graciously declined dessert. She had changed into jeans (she wore a cotton blouse with a denim vest), and she sat with her back to the table edge, pressing her hands to the bench, observing the whole noisy array. She was cool and graceful. I was struck again by her singular presence.

I declined my Italian ice as well.

After dinner there was a dance in a hot wooden room on the second floor. Sitting atop a beat-up chair, a school phonograph played forty-fives. Gentle reader, I must admit this was the first dance I had ever attended. I wish I could say it was pleasant, but everyone seemed acutely nervous. People milled about, uncertain and afraid to dance. There was much discussion about the records. I was staring out a window when Michael spoke to me. (He looked like a miniature yachtsman.)

"There's your heartthrob, Swinburne. Why don't you ask her to dance?"

He nodded toward what was once a stage. Leaning against the proscenium, tapping a foot, was Amy Hart. She was alone.

"Go on," he said.

"I wish I knew how to dance."

He snorted. *"They* know how to dance?"

The couples in the center looked uncomfortable and embarrassed. It seemed as if they were parodying themselves.

"The worst she can say is no," said Michael.

O reader! Wherever I go must it be the same? I live in a nightmare of shyness. I thought that the change of location would have helped, but there I was again. My agonizing shyness was back. It had followed me.

"Ask her!"

"I don't feel like dancing."

"You don't *feel* like dancing!"

I stared at beautiful, lonely Amy and shut my eyes. I cursed myself. I have seldom risen to such a pitch of self-loathing. I repeated to myself, "What is the matter with you?" It was the simplest thing in the world. Just walk fifteen feet and say, "Amy, would you like to dance?" That's all it was, yet I was riveted to my spot. I promised myself I would ask after the next song.

Five songs later I still stood there, hopelessly. O my gentle reader, I stood among a hundred people in the hot, dancing room and felt completely alone and utterly miserable. I asked myself, "When are you going to change? When are you going to grow up?" I had a thousand rational answers and a thousand rational reasons for pushing her out of my life. But I loved her. Amy. Amy. It was the one theme in my life. I felt I was descending deeper and deeper into hopelessness. O Amy, lovely Amy, do you understand? (She still leaned against the proscenium of the stage.) Leslie Shapiro, in red, had entered the room and was hungrily darting her eyes about. My aching head was clamped in iron. I mumbled something to Michael, and I fled that horrible place.

The night air was cooler, and it eased the awful pressure in my brain. How could a body so physically frail contain so much anguish? What is the threshold of pain that one is expected to stand? I am young. I've only been on the planet fourteen years. How can life be so awful and so hopeless in so short a time?

My nocturnal ramblings brought me back eventually to my cabin, where Keating, Michael, and a few others were sitting on bunks, rating all the girls on the field trip. They were deciding whom they would sleep with if they had the chance. Keating sat on the top bunk and acted as a sort of master of ceremonies, sweeping us all within the scope of his huge, acned arms. The room was lit by only a small ceiling bulb.

"Vicki Milne," said Michael. "That's my kind of girl."

"Too short," said Keating.

"Not for me, *baaaa*by," said Michael. "And great legs."

"She does have terrific legs."

"Man," said Michael. "I want to grab her ass."

"Heather Karl," said Keating. "Now there's a prospect for me."

"You wish," said Michael.

"Yeah?"

"Heather Karl is everybody's dream," called out somebody.

"And I can think of two good reasons," added Michael.

"I've got good taste," said Keating. "I already went out with her once."

"And you *know* what they say," said Michael. "The breast is yet to come."

I groaned.

"All right, Romeo," said Keating. "Who do you want to sleep with?"

The shadows turned to hear my answer. In my mind I saw Amy Hart sitting at dinner, her back to the table edge. Her pale, intelligent face. Her silver chain. I had to say something. Michael might blurt it out.

"I don't know," I said. "Heather Karl sounds pretty good to me."

"Get in line, boy!" said Keating. "At least you've got good taste."

"And you *know* what they say . . ." said Michael.

I thought of Heather Karl, a large, horsy girl. She was fourteen and looked as if she were in college. She was frighteningly exuberant, frighteningly athletic, and frighteningly stupid. She was the perfect girl for Keating. They could sit together at football games.

Someone knocked at the door and said, "Lights out in fifteen minutes."

I was far too restless to sleep. I went out and sat for a while on the cabin's steps. Behind me they were still talking about women.

"Andrea Gilpen," someone suggested.

"Too skinny," said Michael.

"Amy Hart."

"What a snob!"

"Yeah," said Keating. "She's a goddamned snob."

I wondered if Keating was so quick to brand her a snob because she was intelligent enough to see through his shallowness. (Sweet Amy, you have one defender always.)

"She's pretty, though," someone said.

"Yeah, but she's so stiff," insisted Keating. "It always looks like she's posing for a goddamned picture."

"I go with Heather Karl," came another voice.

"She's the one for me," said Keating.

O Amy, they were getting into bed now. I could hear suitcases unfastening and ancient wooden drawers creaking. But I was haunted. The night called me. (I like the night because it makes me invisible.) The lights were going out. Michael stood in the door frame.

"Whatcha doing, bro?"

"I'm going for a walk. I don't feel well." Without looking back, I strode into the night.

"I hope you get caught," said Michael.

The wind was up in the forest. Is there music more stirring than the sounds of a forest at night? The rustling leaves bared their pale undersides to the moon. One felt the noisy rush of the breeze, and it was deep dark, hidden dark; it was blue dark to hide the foulest monster and cleanse his soul.

Prophetic reader, you know where I was heading. God help me if I was caught. I kept back along the skirt of the pine trees, far from light, far from life. I passed the empty swimming pool. I passed the social hall. Only a few spotlights burned near the spruce trees (conifers, my learned reader), and these points of light lent a dreamlike effect to the deserted camp. It looked like some vast, ruined civilization. Or perhaps it was an abandoned movie set: all that remained were a few locked buildings. It was a night for dreams. I pushed on. I saw the lights switched out in one last cabin. Quietest of readers, this was the land of the women. Talked about, dreamed about, here they slept in innocent cabins. Here *she* slept: on the top of a bunk bed, I imagined. She would be lying in her sleeping bag with eyes open, her hands behind her head. Most beautiful of women! (And most horrible part of my narrative! I am ashamed, gentle reader, even before I confess what happened next. But like all the truly damned, hopelessly damned, I must confess it all. Nothing can stop me now. I am lost in the deepest, darkest nightmare.)

In silence I moved among the pine trees toward her cabin. All was dark in the camp except for the mad, blowing moon and the few security lights. In the cool blackness you could hear quiet voices. A young woman coughed. A bottle smashed. A light went on briefly then was extinguished. From the forest came the soft sound of night birds. I moved from tree to tree, standing behind each for protection. I was still about one

hundred feet from her cabin. A spotlight fil-
tered down through the branches and cast the
forest in deep shadows that moved gently with
the wind.

I heard voices and I stopped. Female voices.
One laughed. In silence I moved a little closer.
The voices were outside. I peered into the darkness. In front of the cabin, in the gently moving
shadows, were three girls sitting on a blanket
talking. Oh, it was a quiet conversation, gentle
reader! I was still far away, and I dared not move
any closer, but I was sure, I swear I was sure,
that one of them was Amy Hart. There was an
unpleasantly loud, witchlike laugh — Leslie
Shapiro?

God help me, I moved a few trees closer, but
I had to be careful. The crack of a twig might
alert them. I moved on Indian feet. I held the
sides of a rough tree that completely shielded me.
I was now about fifty feet away, and I dared not
move again. It was so dark! But I was convinced
I was in the presence of Amy Hart. (I love you,
Amy.) She sat with her knees drawn up before
her. She seemed to be dressed as I had seen her
before. There was that unmistakable way she
shook her head to adjust her hair! Did you see
it? There was that unmistakable line of her neck.
Leslie (or so it seemed) was sprawled messily on
her stomach, and there was a larger, overweight
girl who was sitting with them.

I kissed my hand and pretended it was Amy's.

I imagined myself on that blanket. I tried to feel the hard ground beneath it. I tried to feel the warmth of Amy Hart near me. I strained to hear their quiet conversation. It was maddeningly impossible. Once, I thought I heard the name "Jim Keating," but I could not be sure. I was so close to them, filled again with a mad, lonely passion. Why was I hiding like this? Amy! I kissed my hand again to pretend it was hers.

I was seized with a desire to get even nearer to her. But I couldn't move; it was too dangerous. I was supposed to be back in my cabin. I couldn't stay any longer, but dear God, I had to. I stared with monster eyes at the shadowy Amy. She ran one hand through her hair. I unbuttoned my shirt. (O reader, burn the manuscript. Stop now, I beg of you.) I removed my burning shirt and laid it on the ground. I removed my sneakers. I paused to listen. A twig snapped under my foot. The moon, too, was moving from behind the trees, and it fell like a guilty beacon on my naked back. But still I could not stop. I removed my brown pants (they were aflame) and placed the sickening things beside my shirt. The forest recoiled at the foulness in its midst. But I had to go on, God help me, I had to. (O Amy, I am sorry that I, who say I love you, must continually hurt you like this.) I stood now in the windy, moon-stricken darkness in just my thin socks and my glowing white underwear. (I cover my eyes with shame as I write this.) I removed the hideously burdened underwear and stood against a tree in just my pathetic socks. I could smell my own madness. I could feel the nauseating heat from my body. And, dear God, I *had* to move closer. I moved to another tree! And another! My clothes receded behind me. I could hear the women speaking in the darkness. My wretched heart was pounding. What was the matter with me? What sickness was lodged within me? I had to get nearer still. I could not stop myself. Amy, here I am. Amy, I am twenty feet away. Amy, look! Look!

A light went on.

"You girls get in the cabin now," said one of the chaperones.

"Five more minutes," said Leslie.

"Now."

I ran (afraid of the light as insects are) for my pale, skinny, naked, stinking life. O reader, spit on him. He grabs his clothes and runs into the forest for cover. His chest is pounding. He wildly pulls his clothes back on, rumpled, cold, full of sticks. He tears back through the campsite. He passes the empty pool. Shoot him before he does it again. Shoot him before he stands again in the darkness and exposes his wretchedness to the white moonlight. Kill him before it is too late, merciful reader. Jam a shotgun to his throat and blow his animal head off. Then take ten hot showers in a row. He is a fungus-headed, salivating rat carcass. Dear God, dear Amy, what have I done? My handwriting grows smaller and smaller as I write. (I attempt to wipe myself from the face of the earth.) The flashlight trembles on the page. Soon it must be daylight. Please let the morning come soon. Let me out of this nightmare.

6

1:15 P.M. **Friday.** Jubilation! That is the way I feel. And you know my moods are violent. They swing from rock-bottom despair to soaring happiness, but today the omens are favorable; all around me I see signs of benign fortune. The weather is sunny and temperate. A breeze moves gently through this study hall. For some reason a great number of people are absent from school today (including my rival, Alex Lewis). The sparse population and, I suppose, the general feeling that our prison term is nearly over has lent an airy, country-club feel to the place.

Or perhaps what the world and the heavens intuitively understand is the rich anticipation of my attending Amy Hart's surprise party tonight. Dear reader, I rarely go anywhere (except antiquarian book sales), and the combined electricity of attending a party *and* being at close range to Amy Hart has put a giddy, sun-drunk spin on my skittering morning. Is there anything I could not do this morning! I am confident and filled with ambition and hope. (As you see by my dating of this entry, an entire day has passed unmarked and unnoticed. This is deliberate. I fell into such a bitter, sleepless depression over my previous entry — so embarrassing I will never reread it — that I felt a day was needed simply to clear out my head.)

A party, dear reader! Can you imagine? How rich! How filled with the tenderness of youth! And there, standing by the staircase, highball in hand, in a satin opera cloak and top hat . . . Why, isn't that Alexander Preston Sturges Swinburne, celebrated bon vivant and boulevardier? How debonairly he stirs his swizzle stick. How rakishly he cocks his hat, suavely eyeing tonight's debutante, Miss Amy Hart, as she slowly, formally, descends the stairs: a picture of loveliness in pink chiffon, pale, beautiful. She stands demurely in her strapless summer gown. How the men stare and the women lower their eyes in envy. Even the ebullient piano player ceases his wild improvisations and, transfixed in wonder, plays "The Impossible Dream" to accompany her measured descent. Then Alex Swinburne takes her fair hand, kisses it formally ("Ahhh!" the company sigh, "*He* is her special one"), and sweeps her across the well-sanded dance floor in a soaring waltz. They take a carriage home through cobbled streets (illuminated only by pale smudges of gaslight). At the door of her home (where a footman stands holding a flaming sconce), Swinburne suddenly pulls her close to him, her perfume swirling about him.

"And will I see you again, Miss Hart?" he says in a voice surprisingly deep and sonorous for a fourteen-year-old.

"Of course."

Then the bell rings and he goes to algebra.

6:40 P.M. I write to calm my nerves. Every two minutes I go to the front window and look for Michael's mother's car. I check my reflection in the mirror. I am wearing a blue, short-sleeved cotton shirt with white buttons and red stitching. It is, I think, an attractive combination of the serious and the casual, providing an elegant intermingling of nineteenth-century formalism and twentieth-century manic-depressive. The ensemble is vibrantly completed with freshly laundered jeans (stiffly elegant) and desert boots whose laces are decorated with tiny red stars. (Except for the dark thing that inhabits it, it is a presentable outfit.) O reader, I wait at my desk in dizzying nervousness. On the pine wall before me is a framed photograph of Basil Rathbone as Sherlock Holmes. He is examining a marble column with a magnifying glass. O Sherlock! You had your woman — *the* woman, as Watson said. And, dear friend Sherlock, dear companion in lonely railway carriages and misty dogcarts, dear genius of detection, I, too, have my woman. Sherlock, she is *the* woman. Can there ever be another? Tonight is her birthday and farewell party, my London friend. It is a cause of great jubilation. There will be public ceremony, fireworks over the Tower, cheering at Traitor's Gate.

A horn! Lo! A car horn! Dear forsaken manuscript, I may be a changed man when I return.

11:00 P.M. I feel nothing but anger. Oh, how my words come back to hurt me. I read *jubilation,* and I feel like ripping the page to shreds. Never write anything down. It will turn around to mock you viciously. Never admit you are happy, for they will taunt you with it and cut you down. Show nothing to the world; mask every despair, mask every happiness. Walk through the streets like all the others: impassive, defeated, ghost-eyed, heartless, pitiless. Destroy everything of beauty.

Here's the story.

Michael's mother picked me up. We rode in the back of a large, heavily upholstered luxury car. His mother inquired about my parents and said they had to get together soon for bridge. Michael and I sighed in the collective misery of small talk. He sat gnarled and gnomelike on the gray seat; he wore a comically wide tie with large polka dots. He also wore a button with a photograph of W. C. Fields.

"I'll be up till ten o'clock," she said. "I'll give you a ride home until then. If you want to stay out later, you'll have to get a ride with someone else."

"Yeah, yeah," said Michael. He kicked at my wrapped presents on the floor. "Three presents, do you think that's enough?"

"They're not expensive," I said.

But in truth I had spent almost thirty dollars for them. In an attempt to imitate the tastes of Alex Lewis, I had purchased two heavy-metal rock albums (Youth in Asia's *Brain-dead* and Iron Testicles' *Live at Budokan*). I had been embarrassed to purchase them. The store was filled with posters (Deborah Harry in pink underwear), T-shirts, buttons, and bumper stickers (AND ON THE EIGHTH DAY GOD CREATED JIM MORRISON). It was a carnival of teasing sexuality and noise. But I was determined to conform, to win Amy's affection at any price. I paid for the horrible records. There was a store alongside selling art prints, and I felt the necessity of purifying myself somehow by purchasing something beautiful. The store was full of glass and mirrors. Someone was drilling in the back room. I flipped through the bins of cheap reproductions: Nastassia Kinski with a boa constrictor between her legs; a man with a sporty cap leaning against a Rolls Royce: POVERTY SUCKS. The place was an adult version of the record store: a mingling of pornography and vulgar comedy. I grew depressed. Then I saw a print of a girl holding a watering can. I examined it closely. I would be lying if I told you I bought it because it was a Renoir. Gentle reader, I bought it because of her *eyes*. They were Amy's eyes: soft and sparkling, blue, tender. I paid fifteen dollars for those eyes, and I walked home from town laden with more presents than I had ever bought for anyone's birthday in my life.

"What did *you* get her?" I asked.

Michael waved a tiny box wrapped in shiny black paper.

"A charm. The Edison school seal. A seven-fifty piece of crap."

"It's very lovely," said his mother.

Michael gave her the finger behind the seat. (This is what you have to look forward to when you have children, gentle reader.)

Leslie Shapiro lived in a large house on Otisco Drive. It was a street filled with dentists and psychologists. She met us at the door and quickly ushered us in. She glanced somewhat disapprovingly at my three presents and placed them behind the couch in the living room. We were directed down the basement steps into a cool room that was filled with people. The only light was that of a blinking pinball machine. In the near darkness I recognized many faces from school.

"Where the hell have you been?" said Jim Keating.

"My stupid mother had to pick up some crap at the tailor's," said Michael.

"You almost blew the whole party."

"Shhhh," someone said.

"Kiss my ass," said Michael.

Silence fell in the room.

"Let's light the candles."

"Shhhh!"

Fourteen birthday candles were lit on a chocolate cake that had been decorated with a yellow *Amy* (an extravagant tail on the *y*). It cast the room in an orange glow. I must confess, honest reader, that I was happy. I looked around the room, at Jim Keating, at the travel magazines, at a clock from Swissair, at a stylized photograph of the Hollywood sign, at the illuminated pinball machine (Teen-age Goddess), and I was happy.

In the sweet realm of my romantic imagination it seemed as if Amy were arriving just to see me. I visualized her now — en route — passing traffic lights, being driven through the warm, shadowy dusk of town (where lovers stood on the summery brink of a long-dreamed embrace). O Amy! You and I are the Gemini twins — in a land where it is always June, and lilacs scent the lingering twilight forever.

A car door slammed outside.

"Shhhh!"

The doorbell rang. Leslie ran up the stairs and switched on the hall light.

"My folks are going to be a little late," said Leslie. "But everything's on for the concert. How was dinner at Benihana?"

"Oh, dee-*lish*," said Amy.

"You've got to see something, Amy. I've bought you the most incredible gift. Check this out. I've got it set up downstairs."

She turned on the light in the stairway.

The crowd downstairs fell back. The lighted cake was held aloft. Someone smothered a laugh.

Then, dear reader, a hideous travesty! *Amy fell down the stairs.* She shouted in pain. She swore and rubbed her elbow. (How I wanted to run to her!) The lights were switched on. "Surprise!" we shouted. Then we sang "Happy Birthday." She looked dazed. Several people came to her assistance.

And so the party began. We all shook hands with her. "Happy birthday. God, I can't believe you'll be moving in three weeks." She had quickly recovered her poise. She stood by the photograph of the Hollywood sign and looked simply beautiful. (Gentle reader, I keep falling in love with her all over again.) She wore an outfit I sometimes had seen in school: a lavender shirt with a white, frilly collar (to me it had a Shakespearean magic) and a darker lavender skirt. I could see she wore stockings and old-fashioned-looking lavender shoes. By now she was amused by the whole idea of a surprise party. She smiled impishly and rolled her eyes in mock scorn whenever anybody asked, "Were you really surprised?" It struck me for the first time that she was self-conscious about her braces, that she held her hand to her mouth when she smiled. But up close, kind reader, she was even more beautiful than at a distance, for her beauty was tempered with a gentle, self-mocking smile. She brushed back her hair. Her neck was artistry and wonder; it flowed beneath the Shakespearean collar.

Gradually I moved toward her.

"Alex," she said.

(The first time! The first time she had spoken it ever!)

"It's really good of you to come."

I awkwardly held out my hand. She smiled and shook it.

Was there an angel chorus somewhere that sang in divine celebration, or was it just the sound of the pinball machine? Did a supernatural radiance bathe us two and envelop us lovingly in a strange, tingling illumination, or was my foot just asleep? Her hand was warm, and much smaller than I had imagined. I could see the tiny silver chain around her neck. Her eyes were shadowed in a delicate blue. Her complexion was slightly less than perfect when you looked at it very closely. I groped for something original to say, something that would distinguish me from the others and, at the same time, subtly suggest I was in love with her.

"Were you really surprised?" I asked.

"Pretty much," she said. "I think I knew something was up about one second before the lights went on."

I nodded.

"But I can't believe I fell down the stairs. It was *so* queer. I've never done anything like that in my life. It was very embarrassing."

"I thought it was kind of charming."

"I'm glad somebody did." She rubbed her sore elbow theatrically.

"Well, happy birthday," I said. "You've reached the big one-four."

"That's what they say." She turned away. She was bored. "Leslie, people need knives and forks for the cake."

"I'm doing the best I can," said Leslie, running up the stairs.

Amy looked at her watch.

"Do you have to go somewhere?" I said.

"No. I've got to call somebody. Excuse me, will you?"

She moved, tall and stately, through the crowd and disappeared up the steps. Jim Keating scored 50,000 bonus points; the pinball machine lit up red and with a resonant *knock* gave him a free game.

The moment had not gone as I had antici-
pated. There was so much more to say. I had
wanted to be witty, to be enigmatic, to draw her
interest, but I had accomplished nothing. Instead I clearly saw myself standing in a crowd of
identical admirers, all competing for her attention. I sat down on the couch and meditated on
what had gone wrong. (I assumed the telephone
call was to Alex Lewis who I had heard was sick.)
What was unsettling to me was the real physical
attraction I had felt up close — and her complete indifference toward me. If I had felt a
flicker of humor, of dislike even, it would have
given me something to think about. But instead
it was clear that I was simply someone whom she
didn't know very well and probably saw little
reason to *try* to know well.

I was certain that if I could just speak to her
alone, for five minutes, I could begin to tell her
something of the way I felt. Or at least make her
see that there was something in me worth knowing. That's all I needed for tonight: an opening,
a suggestion of complexity. If I could just make
her want to know me a little better, I was sure I
could arrange another meeting. Then there could
be letters. Even if she was moving, I could write
letters. I would pour my heart out without shyness. She would wait with tender delight for these
letters. They would be passionate, magical, and
exceedingly gentle. And every sentence would

mean "I love you, Amy." My love would beam from the pages. It would shine from my signature (simply a heart).

Lavender Amy sat on the living room couch and opened her presents. There was a scarf, an engraved pen, a red paperback called *Love* (she smiled and read the inscription), a pillow with *Amy Hart* artfully embroidered on it, a junior high school charm, and a leather-bound autograph book. She came to the records and carefully opened the wrapping paper as if she were saving it. "Oh," she said and looked at them with a quickness that suggested she already owned them. She glanced at the gift card. She placed them by the pile of other presents. There were a few small things (people were drifting away now), and she finally came to my Renoir print. She slid it from its wrapping paper, looked at it with a smile, examined the gift card, and thanked everyone formally for their kindness. "It's so queer having a party like this," she said. "And it's so queer sort of saying good-bye to everyone. Leslie has my new address in California if anybody wants to write to me. But thank you all for this."

Jim Keating got everyone to sing "Happy Birthday" again. Keating sang it very high and off key and got everyone to laugh, especially Heather Karl. Amy seemed touched by the song, and for a second I thought she might cry. But she just got up from the couch with that self-mocking smile and comic roll of the eyes.

Confused reader, it was all new to me. I felt lost. The painting had meant nothing to her. The records had meant nothing to her. And clearly I meant nothing to her.

I sat in the kitchen drinking orange juice with Michael.

"Aren't you glad you came?" he asked mockingly.

I frowned.

"Did you get to talk to her?"

"A little."

"She's a snob. I told you."

The wooden door to the kitchen was pushed open.

"Oh, *there* you two are," said Leslie. "I was looking all over for you. Can you help me clear up downstairs before my folks get home?"

There were only six of us left in the living room. The wrapping paper had been thrown away; the presents had been neatly stacked by the mail table. I sat with Leslie Shapiro on the flowered couch. Keating and Heather Karl sat on the white rug. Michael stood scowling by the fireplace. Amy sat in a modern metal chair next to him.

"So where will you be living in California?" I asked.

"Beverly Hills. That sounds so queer, doesn't it? *Beverly Hills.* Coldwater Canyon Drive. I haven't seen it but my father says it's really lovely.

The house supposedly belonged to one of the Beach Boys. And, hey, in one year I'll be going to Beverly Hills High School. That's a classy alma mater, isn't it?"

The phone rang. It was for Leslie.

"I'm going for a walk," said Amy. "Anybody want to come?"

"I do," I said (perhaps too quickly).

It was a sweet-scented June night when I found myself walking alone with Amy Hart down Otisco Drive. I could not believe my luck. I, who had stood two nights ago in trembling nakedness not twenty feet from her, was now walking beside her — the woman I had spent so many months dreaming of. I was rapturously happy. She was really here. She was Amy Hart. She was five feet away. I could touch her by simply reaching out an arm. I repeated in my head: I love you, Amy; I love you, Amy; I love you, Amy. I wanted her to know. I remembered my promise: *whatever the consequences I would tell her.* I had to tell her before she left.

"Did you like the painting?" I asked.

"What's that?"

"The girl with the watering can. That was my present."

"Oh, it was pretty."

(Dear God, I felt myself losing control again.)

"I bought it because the eyes reminded me of yours."

"Really. That's so queer."

"There's something about the paleness of the skin, too, that reminded me of you."

(Careful!)

"I'll have to look at it."

The street was windy and dark. A few houses were lit. We had reached the end of the block; we headed back.

"Amy, there's something I want to tell you."

"Yeah?"

I love you, I love you, I love you, I love you, I love you, I love you, I love you, I love you, I love you, I love you, I love you, I love you.

"This is going to sound pretty odd to you. Pretty *queer* as you might say."

She laughed.

(Oh, I was wild! My head was going to explode.)

"For a long time now . . ."

"Yeah?"

She was looking at me. Alone in the warm dark she was beautiful and she was Amy and she was looking at me. I wanted to kiss her; how I wanted to take her in my arms and say, "I love you, Amy. I've loved you for a year. I've wanted you. I've dreamed of you. I've called your house. I've waited for this night." *But I couldn't say it.* Amy, help me. *You've got to know.*

My voice was weak.

"I . . . really wish you happiness . . . in California."

"Thank you, Alex."

No! No!

I suddenly heard Michael calling out into the night.

"Swinburne! Where are you?"

"Here!" I called.

"Hurry up, my mother's coming. She's giving everybody a ride."

"Okay," I said.

"Great," said Amy.

Goddamn me! Goddamn me! Detestable reader, goddamn me for the puny, goddamned terrified fool that I am. Goddamn me! Three weeks! Three weeks and she will be gone! *She has got to know.*

7

Morning. Evening. I've been sick in bed for three school days. I am delirious. I have a fever. I vomited last night at the foot of my bed, and the room stinks of illness. Dear God, am I losing my mind? Where is she? Where is she? They've all been here to visit: Michael, Leslie, even Keating, but not her. She is the only one I want to see! O Amy, I am losing control. Where are you? Come to my bedside. Come wake me with a kiss. (Don't you know the Sleeping Death can only be cured by the kiss of one's own true love?) Someday my princess will come. I know, dear God, she will. Amy Hart. Amy Hart. Mary Hat. Army Hat. Someday my Hart will come. Will come with her army hat. Amy. Amy. My Amy. My heart. My aim is heart. My Hart is true. Amy Goddess. Come kiss me, Amy. Stand by my fevered bedside. Let me draw you into my sickness my horror let me hold you with my horror my heart. O God my handwriting is wild running across the pages sense gone only scrawl only Amy only God let me sleep let me just sleep.

Later. Morning. I feel as if I am dehydrating. It must be morning because *Morning Edition* is on the radio. "I'm Carl Kassel, Bob Edwards is on vacation this week." I switch the stations blindly. The red digital numbers burn into my skull. An old song: "Too Busy Thinking About My Baby." I listen to song lyrics for some answer. My poor head throbs on the pillow. I twist the dial again. "I'm Carl Kassel; Bob Edwards is on vacation this week." It drones on and on. I lie in a stinking sweat. My skull is clamped in a vise of fungus. O Amy, your ghost fills this lonely room. My poor mother just came upstairs and held my hand. Can she ever forgive me?

I take aspirin to bring down the fever. And outside my room, the blasting, bright, sun-swamped world walks healthily by in a kind of dream.

Night. In the secrecy of my cell I listen to Dr. Ruth's *Sexually Speaking*. O God, the world is even sicker than I am. I hear the obscene nervousness in the callers' voices. They air their hungry desires before a million bedroom ears. In my fever I imagine I call.

"Dr. Ruth?"

"Yes."

"This is Anthony from Staten Island." (I need the fictive guise in case my mother is listening.) "First, I want to say how much I enjoy your program."

"Thank you very much, Anthony! Are you using contraceptives?"

"No, Dr. Ruth, my question concerns —"

"Then I *don't* want to talk to you!"

"But, Dr. Ruth, my question is about —"

"I'm sorry, but I don't want to talk to you unless you're using contraceptives."

"All *right*. I'm using contraceptives."

"Good, Anthony. Now what is your question?"

"I'm fourteen years old. And I'm in love with a girl in my class. But I can't talk to her. I just can't break through my shyness."

"Tell me, Anthony, what are you so afraid of?"

"I'm not sure."

"Okay, you're afraid, Anthony. There's nothing wrong with that. Love is a *very* frightening thing. But tell me, are you happy with the current state of your relationship?"

"No."

"So what do you have to lose by telling her?"

"I don't know. I'm just so scared."

"But, Anthony, what do you have to lose?"

". . . I guess nothing."

"You're right! You have absolutely nothing to lose! She may like you. And even if she doesn't, at least you asked! Now, Anthony, will you do me a favor?"

"Sure."

"Will you talk to her?"

"I'll try."

"No. No. I want you to say to me, 'Dr. Ruth, I promise I will talk to her.' Will you say that for me?"

"All right. Dr. Ruth, I promise I will talk to her."

"Okay. Now say it one more time."

"Dr. Ruth, I promise I will talk to her."

"Good boy. And you'll drop us a card, Anthony, to let us know what happened?"

"Sure."

"You have my address?"

"Yes."

"Okay, good luck to you, Anthony."

"Thank you, Dr. Ruth."

Trace the call. Break down his door. Turn floodlights on his sweaty face. Fingerprint the phone. Compare the voiceprints in front of a jury. "Your Honor, the prints clearly match. We've found out who the monster is. He is sitting in this courtroom." "You don't mean . . . ?" "Yes, Your Honor, I call Alexander Preston Sturges Swinburne to the stand."

"Tell me, Mr. Swinburne, how long have you known my client, Miss Amy Hart?"

"I've known her for about a year."

"A year, I see. And may I ask if you are in love with my client?"

"I'm . . . not sure."

"Isn't it true that you've *called* my client, Mr. Swinburne? Isn't it true you've often called her house four or five times a night?"

"I don't remember."

"Will the clerk bring Mr. Swinburne's phone bills before the court?"

"I *may* have called once or twice, casually."

"Once or twice! Casually! And spending thirty dollars on my client's birthday, Mr. Swinburne, would you call that *casually* as well?"

"I don't know." (God, give me a rest.)

"And I have one more piece of evidence, Mr. Swinburne. A letter written in Spanish that you mailed to my client."

"I don't know Spanish."

"Will the clerk bring Mr. Swinburne's school records before the court?"

"Okay, I know a little Spanish."

"Two years of Spanish? Mr. Swinburne, would you call two years of Spanish a *little?*"

"I don't know it well."

"You received A's in Spanish, Mr. Swinburne. Would you describe straight A's as *not knowing it well?*"

"Please leave me alone."

"Why, are we *bothering* you, Mr. Swinburne? Are we bothering the beast who sent an obscene note to my client, who, I remind this jury, is a goddess? I'll read it to you."

"Please don't."

"Oh, I must. Written on blue paper. *Amy:*

Quiero dormir contigo. (I want to sleep with you.)
Do you deny writing this note, Mr. Swinburne?"

". . . I never mailed it."

"We found it, Mr. Swinburne. We found it in
the garbage can in Room 208. I believe you have
study hall in Room 208?"

"I never wrote it."

"And who stole the swimsuit issue of *Sports Illustrated* from the Edison Junior High School library this year, Mr. Swinburne?"

"I don't know."

"And who stood naked in the moonlight on the
biology field trip, Mr. Swinburne?"

"I don't know."

"And who dreams of Amy Hart's bra strap, Mr.
Swinburne?"

"I don't know."

"And who is the most vile excuse for a human
being who has ever degraded the earth with his
sick, pathetic presence? Tell the jury, Mr. Swinburne. Answer the jury, Mr. Swinburne. Who is
the most wretched, pathetic animal in this world,
Mr. Swinburne?"

. . . I don't know, I swear I don't know. My
green pajamas are soaked with sweat. I drink a
gallon of water every hour. I take penicillin pills
every six hours, and they dry my brain. I fill the
room with a sour, acid smell. Cool breeze from
somewhere. Please, God, let it stay. Just let me
sleep. Take me away.

"So why are you torturing yourself, Alex?"

"I love her, Dr. Ruth."

"But what good is torturing yourself? Talk to her! Invite her to a movie. Take her out for a soda."

"I want to, but I can't."

"What do you have to lose?"

"Nothing. Nothing."

"Promise me you're going to talk to her."

"I promise I'm going to talk to her."

"The saddest words, Alex, are 'would have,' 'could have,' and 'should have.' "

Daylight. Still no sleep. Noon whistle. I take a shower. I must get some air. I fumble with my clothes and stagger down the stairs on unsteady legs.

"Where are you going, Alex?" asks my mother. She is reading at the kitchen table.

"I just need a walk."

"I don't think you should be out of bed."

"I'm mailing a letter, that's all."

The screen door slams behind me, and I'm out in the dizzying light of afternoon. The elementary school children are walking home for lunch. My legs are weak. The world is running light, streaming, unfocused. My dear helpless God, I cannot live among all this light and beauty and youth. "So why are you torturing yourself?" asks my reflection in a car window.

I end up back in my room.

I watch the junior high school girls through the window. They are so self-assured, so beautiful. I watch as if I were a distant, imprisoned creature behind bars. I claw the window of my cell.

"Alex, Leslie is here," my mother calls up.

I hear footsteps on the stair. I sink back on my bed.

"Hi, how you feeling?"

I let loose a long, melodramatic moan.

"Oh," she says. "It's pity-me-I'm-going-to-die week on the four-thirty movie."

"Ha ha."

"Guess what?"

I hold a hand to my forehead. "What?"

"Mrs. H. asked when you were coming back."

Leslie sits on my reading chair. Her black hair is too long and rather messy. She wears a zebra-striped dress.

"Tell her she can rent my desk."

"I've got your homework."

"I stand gasping on my deathbed and you bring me homework?"

"What do you want me to bring?" she says.

The words fall from my lips before I can stop them.

"Amy Hart."

She looks up. (Dear God, I *am* losing my mind.) "What?"

"That was a nice party you gave for her . . ."

The words catch in my throat.

"I'm glad you came."

". . . Thanks for inviting me."

But the words had leaked out. I was breaking down. The inner world (so mad, so infernally guilty) was cracking through the shell. She knew what I had said. She knew exactly what was on my mind. (Dear Leslie, I am sorry. I apologize for what can never be retracted.)

She left.

Night fell on the island. I kept the lights out in my cramped cell. Dear God, the sweating started again. I changed my stinking pajamas. I took my penicillin with shaking hands. I lay with my eyes open, my head back on the pillow, chanting "Amy, Amy, Amy, Amy." Michael had told me that she had gone to the beach with Alex Lewis. (O calendar brother, why have you forsaken me?) Coldwater Canyon Drive, Beverly Hills, California. Amy, Amy, Amy, I will fly to Los Angeles; I'll steal; I'll do anything. I want to take you in my arms. I want to hold you: white moccasins, woolen socks with two-inch cranberry stripes, lavender shirt with white Shakespearean collar, tiny silver chain. Your straight short hair and your self-mocking smile and your braces. I want to hear you say, "It's so queer." Make me whole, Amy.

I had to call her now. The phone number lived

in my fingertips. In two and a half weeks she'd be gone.

I found the desk light. Dialed. I hung up after the first ring.

O God, what time was it? Was it the middle of the night? What day was it?

I had to talk to her. Before she went I had to let her know. *Quiero dormir contigo.* Amy, I am sorry for my wretchedness. You cannot sleep with an angel. You can only adore an angel. Her white Indian moccasins! Her warm small hand! Did I tell you, reader, that I touched her hand once? She shook my hand at the party. No, I'm not dreaming. O Amy, what have I got to lose? What have I got to lose? The night, the torturing night, is thick in my throat. I sweat through five pairs of pajamas a night. Sour, acid sweat. The penicillin is making me hallucinate.

How many more nights am I going to lie here in misery? How many more months of my life am I going to spend dreaming of her? How much longer? Grow up, Alex. Get out of this nightmare.

I was ready to vomit with nervousness.

I took the phone and dialed.

"Yello?" came her father's voice.

I cleared my throat. "May I speak with Amy Hart, please?"

"May I ask who's calling?"

(Lie, lie!) "Alex Swinburne. I'm a friend of hers from school."

"Okay . . . Amy!"

(Hang up. Hang up and run away.)

Another extension was lifted.

I was pouring with sweat.

"Hello?"

Her goddess voice; I could not speak.

"Hello?" she said again.

"Amy, this is Alex Swinburne."

"Wow. I was just thinking about you."

"Really?" (I love you, Amy.)

"Yeah, I was looking at that painting you gave me, and I remember you saying you thought the eyes looked like mine."

"Don't they?" I held my hand to my burning forehead.

"I think they kind of do." She laughed. "It's funny how it's so difficult to see yourself objectively. I mean, I would never have noticed it if you hadn't pointed it out."

"Oh."

"So how are you? You're sick or something, right?"

"Oh, it's nothing."

"It's so queer. Everybody I know is sick. This is really a pretty painting though, Alex. I'm looking at it right now. It's really striking, you know? There's something almost mesmerizing in that girl's face. It's the first thing you look at when you come into the room."

(It's your face, Amy! Can't you see it?) "I . . . I'm having a party at my house," I stammered, wildly improvising. (O God, what would my mother say!)

"When is it?"

"It's . . . Friday. It's a week from Friday . . . I wanted to know if you could make it?" (No, no, no, no.)

"Yeah. I don't see why not. What time?"

"Oh, I don't know . . . eight, nine. Whenever you can."

"You live on that street by the park, right?"

"Right."

"Okay, I'll see you then. I gotta go now, all right? My father's calling me."

"All right. Thanks. I'll see you, Amy."

She hung up.

"I love you."

I replaced the phone and shut off the light. The shutters blew back in the wind.

"Alex, shut the windows up there. There's going to be a storm," called my mother.

"Okay," I said.

But I didn't get up. My head was suddenly clear. The room was cold. I pulled up the top sheet and held it to my cheeks.

Dear reader, I didn't know what to think. I had called her up; I had invented a party, and she had accepted. And she liked the painting. "Mesmerizing," she had said. "It's so difficult to see yourself objectively." (The girl was brilliant. There was no question of that.) And she had been thinking of me. And she had accepted my invitation!

Gentle reader, I was shivering. And I realized I was scared.

It was so queer.

8

1:20 P.M. Monday. I invited Michael, Leslie, and Jim Keating as well.

Now all I had to do was reveal my plan to my parents. (They are difficult people, understanding reader, and I have not written much about them because they hate me enough already — well, perhaps they don't hate me as much as realize that The Stranger Walks Among Them.

This is a sad, lonely world! I suppose that's why people try so desperately hard to fall in love. If their lives can be redeemed by an Amy Hart, then perhaps their sadness is diminished. (Have you noticed how all my philosophical speculation eventually leads to Amy Hart? This is what is known as an obsessive personality.) But my parents had to be told of the party. The difficulty is that not only have I never had a party at my house, but I've never even invited a woman to my house. (Depressing and solitary admission!)

And what if my mother said no? Or what if my father viciously snapped, "There'll be no parties in this house. Your brothers gave enough parties here. We've done our share"?

Dear reader, I sit in study hall and look about and wonder. (Alex Lewis is absent again today. Hooray! Perhaps he is undergoing brain surgery. Perhaps I can call the operating room at a critical juncture and startle the surgeon so he drops the brain on the floor. "Nurse, would you pick that up, please?") Friendly reader, I am nervous. My legs tingle. I sit here with an air of boredom, but inside I am filled with anticipation. I stare at the bulletin board filled with photographs and cartoons from World War I, and I imagine asking my mother about the party.

A sunny parlor. It is filled with flowers. **MOTHER** *(young, buoyant) stands at an easel painting a burgundy rose.* **ALEX** *walks on. He is wearing a tuxedo. One of his arms is missing. His demeanor suggests world-weariness.*

ALEX: Mother?

MOTHER: Yes, love?

ALEX *(sitting at the white metal table, toying idly with a war medal):* I was thinking about a party Friday night. Is the idea just too awful?

MOTHER: Oh, dear, another one?

ALEX: If you and Father wouldn't mind.

MOTHER: Oh, Alex . . . *(She sighs.)* You

97

know Father and I are worried about you. This mad, reckless life you lead: the champagne parties, the midnight swims, the jazz bands.

ALEX: I am sinful, Mother.

MOTHER: I didn't want to mention it, but your father was rather hoping you'd be thinking about entering the firm by now. That's what you always said you wanted to do . . . And you've been home three weeks.

ALEX: Oh, Mother! Can't you see the war has changed all that? The war has changed everything.

MOTHER: But how long can you go on like this, Alex? The parties, the dancing, the drinking? Surely it must seem rather empty to you.

ALEX: Oh, Mother, I fill up my days with drinking to mask the insufferable pain I feel in just living.

MOTHER: It's that girl you're keen on, isn't it?

ALEX *(softly):* Yes, Mother.

MOTHER: She is rather pretty.

ALEX: Oh, Mother, she is everything in the world to me! Yet, how could she ever love me . . . a cripple!

MOTHER: Oh, Alex! *(She puts her arm on his shoulder.)*

ALEX: Just this last party, Mother. Just this last party and I know I can win her heart.

MOTHER *(compassionately):* Dear Alex, of course you may have the party. *(She claps her hands.)* Alex! Let's give the grandest party that this poor old town has ever seen! What do you think?

ALEX: Do you mean it?

MOTHER: We'll redecorate the whole place! We'll fill it with flowers and wine and candles! Oh, Alex. *(She takes his hand.)* Together we'll win the heart of your fair young maiden! I *know* we will!

ALEX: I do love you, Mother.

4:00 P.M. My mother stood peeling potatoes in the kitchen. It was late afternoon.

"What's new at school?" she asked.

"Do you think I could have a party here on Friday night?"

She stopped. She thought a moment. She smiled gently.

"I think it's a great idea."

(I do love you, Mother!)

It was that easy. I said thanks and went out for a walk. Most wonderful day! I wanted to clap my hands. I wanted to shout "Hooray!" And Amy was coming! Sweet, beautiful Amy of the Renoir eyes! In my very own house. O reader, it was nothing short of wonderful. I had a mad idea, as I kicked along the streets, of calling Michael, Leslie, and Keating and telling them that the party was canceled. Then Amy would come alone to the door.

ALEX THE HIPSTER *(in Hawaiian shirt, gold chains, toupee):* Like, hey, girl, the others have, like, split, you know?

AMY *(blonde, tanned):* Wow. That's, like, so queer.

ALEX THE HIPSTER: So maybe it's, like, you and me, you know? Catch some rays. Drive the Jag up to Malibu. I got some business with Spielberg, you know?

O Amy, I see you before me on this spring day. Cartwheels and handsprings! I pass the playground and I see you on the swings: your pale forehead, your half-smile. You pull your hair back over your ears, shake your head to the wind.

Do you, Alexander Preston Sturges Swinburne, take this woman, Amy Hart, to be your lawfully wedded wife?

I do.

To cherish?

I do.

To give some meaning to your life?

I do.

You may kiss the bride.

(Such sweetness! Such melting sweetness!)

I now pronounce you monster and goddess.

And then I am transformed. The scales fall away. The pointed fingernails recede. The face reverts from hideous distortion to modest boy-ishness. I grow in height. I fill out. Something black and horrid is pulled from my scalp and in-cinerated. (Dear God, I can breathe again!) I speak to strangers. Amy holds my hand in school. We're seen together. We dance. We're in the school play as the young lovers Alroy and Felic-ity. We kiss at the finale in a long, deeply felt embrace. The audience weeps, smiling.

5:00 P.M. Thursday. O joyous reader, I write less and less as I feel happier and happier. Only twenty-six hours to go. I keep imagining how it will be. And I am a diligent host. I have ar-ranged with my dear, sweet mother to have a variety of foods including her delicious mush-room hors d'oeuvres, in short, all the accoutre-ments of a successful soiree. I have planned for every contingency. For guests who are easily bored I have rented (or rather my father has rented) a video cassette of *The List of Adrian Mes-senger.* Forgetful reader, do you not remember it is my favorite film? Do you not remember the unmasking scene at the end? (The gypsy stable-man is Frank Sinatra!) I am ready. I am ready. I am ready.

Come, night!

1:25 P.M. Friday. June 17. (All wonderful things happen on dates with a 3, 7, or 9, especially a 7.) Study hall. My hands shake. I sit here amid a pile

101

of books and the homework I'm supposed to be doing, but I can't concentrate on any of it. My handwriting is atrocious. I can hardly hold the pen still. I can't write down the words fast enough.

Dear reader, I must slow down. I must concentrate. There now, observe the neatness of my handwriting. Each letter is printed in minute, intense, heavily pressed character. My handwriting indicates that I am in complete control. (Except that my hand is killing me from squeezing the pen so hard.) I spoke to Amy in the hall after Spanish.

"You haven't forgotten about the party?" I said.

In an amused tone she said, "No, I *haven't* forgotten." Then she moved down the hall in a hurry. To watch her is to see how far apart we still are. But she does acknowledge that I exist. That's something new. When I walk by her in the hall she often gives me a small wave of recognition. (I am grateful for even that.)

Leslie saw me at lunch and asked if she could do anything for the party. I felt like saying, "Yeah, don't show up." But of course I did not. In truth, her friendship (argumentative and confusing as it is) has been somewhat flattering. She likes me too much; I like her too little — but I don't have very many friends. I appreciate the few who care.

Do you recall, gentle reader, the sad dedication of Poe's *Eureka?* It is the story of my life. I often speak the words when out on my walks. "To the few who love me and whom I love — to those who feel rather than to those who think — to the dreamers and those who put faith in dreams as in the only realities — I offer this Book of Truths . . ." The words move me deeply. They speak of such a lonely life. If ever I write the sad, solitary book of my heart, that must be the epigraph: ". . . the dreamers and those who put faith in dreams as in the only realities . . ." I do believe in dreams. What else is there to believe in? I believe in Amy Hart, in her beauty, and in the essential goodness of her heart. (And yes, cynical reader, these words mock me with their absurdity. Yes, I don't even know her.)

I am confused, somewhat frightened. All I long for is the chance to open my heart to Amy. Somehow these past few days have made me feel that she cares for me in small ways. This, too, I know you will laugh at. But I believe there is a connection between us. I've been feeling there's some kind of emotional link. I suppose that's all I want from my party: to reach out a hand . . . I do love you, Amy. If only you'd let me share it.

A walk might be an effective strategy to see her alone tonight. Or perhaps I can find a quiet corner of the house. If all else fails, I'll at least ask her to the movies. It'll be a way to extend whatever inroads I've made (of love? of friendship?). As I write I find myself growing calmer. Dear

103

Amy, what are you doing now? Are you nervous about this evening? Are you looking at yourself in the mirror, or are you beyond that kind of vanity? To me, dear Amy, you would always be beautiful. Where do you come from, sweet Amy? How I long to explore the mystery of who you are.

It is eight P.M. I am sitting downstairs in the living room writing. I feel too nervous to do anything else. I sit on the couch in the glow of a glass-globed lamp. The clock ticks loudly in the hall. The house smells of baking. On the dining-room table are neat rows of breads, biscuits, and cheeses. On a small wheeled cart by the clock are fat liters of soda, swollen with gas. My mother (I had hoped she might be going out tonight) fusses in the kitchen. She looks rather dressed up for the occasion. My father is also in the kitchen, with his glasses on, reading bank pamphlets, figuring the math on a tiny calculator. They speak softly. Now I hear ice dropped into a glass.

"What time do you expect them, Alex?" calls my mother.

"I said around eight. But I told Michael to be here early."

"I don't know if we're going to have enough mushroom hors d'oeuvres."

The clock continues to tick. It chimes the quarter hour. I hear a car outside. There are voices. They pass. (Michael told me to expect a few crashers to show up.)

"You sure they got the day right?" asks my father.

"I'm sure."

My father walks into the living room and picks at some grapes. He sits on the love seat by the window.

"What are you always writing?" he asks.

"Homework," I say.

"They sure give you a lot of it."

"I have hard courses."

"I wish your brothers had a little of your self-discipline."

I observe my father. We are two males who are waiting. He looks tired. It's only recently, I reflect, that I've begun to see my parents as human beings. It's kind of sad.

The clock chimes the half hour.

"They'll be here any minute," says my father.

He gets up, and I adjust myself on the couch. It feels as if my clothes are wilting. (I'm wearing freshly laundered jeans and my sporty blue shirt with the red stitching. I mention the outfit so perceptive readers can see that I've duplicated what I wore to Leslie's party. I am a great believer in luck.)

I wander into the kitchen and drink some water. The light is on in the upper oven. On an aluminum tray sit the hors d'oeuvres. The clock ticks. *No one is coming.*

The clock chimes eight forty-five. Then it chimes nine o'clock.

I am feeling sick.

I go upstairs. I write now on my bed, my old imprisoning cell. And I was sure that I had finally escaped from it. On the bed is the receipt from Video Village for *The List of Adrian Messenger*. If I had the stomach I suppose I could go downstairs and watch it alone, as I've always done in the past. What a ghastly joke it all is. There is a lesson to be learned here. Never allow yourself to hope for even one thing. My room feels like desolation, like a solitary Christmas. Downstairs, my mother has put on the stereo to make the house seem less empty. I am ready to cry. How dare I hope for anything?

The clock chimes nine-fifteen.

O dear God, is it all starting again? I am sick to my stomach. Someone's coming up the stairs. By the footsteps, it is my mother. She knocks.

"Alex?" she says softly.

I steel myself to keep from crying.

"Yes?"

She opens the door.

"Do you think you should call Michael?"

"I — I don't know."

"I think you should."

"Maybe I will."

She seems ready to speak some words like "I'm sorry," but she turns down the stairs. I hear her steps fade into the music from the stereo.

Amy, how could you do this to me?

I shut my eyes and try to sleep. Downstairs my father and mother are talking. I hear a car outside. A door slams.

"Alex!" my father calls. "Somebody's here."

9

Michael and Leslie were downstairs. Michael had brought some records. With their presence at least it couldn't be a complete humiliation.

"Big crowd," said Michael.

"They heard you were coming."

My parents shook hands with Leslie Shapiro. She was wearing a garish neo-punk combination of red and blue. We sat in the living room talking about school and vacation.

"Anybody want to start *The List of Adrian Messenger?*" I asked.

"I think wait till more people show up," said Leslie.

Michael snorted. "You wish."

"Thanks, bro," I said.

"Face it, Swinburne, you're the kiss of death."

"And you're the big social success, huh?"

"Well, I was until I met you."

"I see."

"And then," he said (warming to his subject), "your black shadow spread over me." He held his hands out expressively. Then he laughed.

"You two are great fun," said Leslie.

The doorbell rang. It was Jim Keating and his amazon, Heather Karl.

It slowly began to feel more like a party. I was relieved. My parents delicately disappeared. About five more people arrived; I had not invited them, but they were friends of Keating's.

Michael's records were soon playing; the guests were talking. Yet I felt quite alone and rather irrationally melancholy. I sat in the kitchen by myself and looked at the clock. I shut my eyes and listened to the drifting voices of the others. My ears were ringing. I tried to shake the sadness. Even if Amy wasn't coming, there was no reason not to be happy. People were enjoying themselves. But she had told me she was coming. I had reminded her of the time. Maybe she just forgot.

"Alex?"

It was garish, hopeful Leslie.

"Are you all right?"

"Yeah. I'm okay."

"What are you doing in here all alone?"

"Brooding."

"Do you mind if I sit down?"

"If you want."

She studied the green polish on her fingernails.

"You know, Michael's probably going to kill me for saying this," she said, "but he told me in the car that you're in love with Amy Hart."

(The deceitful bastard.)

"I wouldn't say in 'love,' " I said, averting my eyes.

"That's what he said."

"Is it really any concern of yours?"

"Well, I don't want to hurt you, Alex. I wouldn't do that for anything. But I thought you should know she's got a boyfriend."

"I know that . . . Alex Lewis . . . I know all about that."

"Okay, I'm sorry. I just didn't want to see you hurt."

"That's awfully kind of you."

"You don't have to snap."

"Was I snapping?"

"Why are you so bitter, Alex?"

"Why are you so sweet?"

"I'm not."

"What *are* you then?"

"You know, you are really a pain in the ass sometimes."

She got up and walked back into the living room.

I sat there in anger and confusion. Why the hell was I so mean? I was spitting in the face of every kindness that came my way. And for what? For Amy Hart? I held my head in my hands. I had to clear her out of my mind. But how could

I? Amy. Amy. *I want to touch you tonight.* The records were louder; the laughter more raucous. I joined the others in the living room. It was noisy. Leslie was sitting alone on the love seat.

"Leslie, I'm sorry. Would you drink a toast?" I said, raising my ginger ale.

"To what?" she asked.

The doorbell rang. The room fell strangely silent. The screen door opened and there stood Amy Hart. (The toast stuck in my throat.) She was beautiful. She wore a white short-sleeved shirt with black and red pinstripes. On her neck I could see her tiny silver chain. A rough black belt and cranberry trousers, striped socks and her white Indian moccasins. (O Amy!) Her face was fresh and alive. She had one hand in her back pocket, and she eyed the assembly with that glorious, self-mocking smile.

I stood frozen. And a moment later Alex Lewis came in behind her. He put his hand on her shoulder. He wore shorts and a football jersey.

I nearly dropped my drink. Who the hell had asked him to show up? I had thought he was sick. What was he doing in my house? What was he doing standing in my living room, with his arm around Amy Hart? Jesus Christ, I had invited *her*. I had asked *her*. She had agreed to come. She had been thinking of me when I called. She had loved the painting. She had seen the similarities in the eyes. She had waved to me in the hall. There was a link between us . . .

"A toast to what?" said Leslie.

I turned to her. The color was draining from my face.

"Uh . . . to you," I said.

She smiled a little confusedly.

"And to you," she said.

We tapped plastic glasses.

What was Alex Lewis doing in my house? The nerve of him! I couldn't ask him to leave. But it was impossible to have him there.

Amy circulated easily. She met me by the soda cart.

"Thanks for asking me, Alex."

"Oh, sure."

"You need some more ice."

I went into the kitchen. Jim Keating was kissing Heather. I threw my hands to my eyes, muttered, "Sorry," and backed out.

In the living room, Alex Lewis was telling a story about how the Edison soccer team got drunk when they went to Canada for the competition.

There was a hand on my arm. My mother was smiling. "Everybody seems to be having such a good time," she said.

Amy sat on the footstool, laughing at Lewis's story. Her eyes were filled with love for him.

"And then Unger puked out the seventh-floor window of the hotel!" said Lewis. "All the way down to the street. You could hear it. Splat! Right on the sidewalk."

Amy laughed.

Michael and a few others had started *The List of Adrian Messenger,* but no one was paying attention.

"Have you ever seen this movie?" I said to Amy.

"What?"

"This is a good movie. Have you —"

She wasn't even listening to me. She was smiling at Lewis.

"So he puked out the window. And, like, we all thought he was done. But no. He turns around. He wipes his face. And then he pukes all over the bed! It was the most disgusting thing I've ever seen. He'd had spaghetti for dinner. So it's this red spaghetti sauce all over the bed!"

Amy was beside herself with laughter.

The movie blared to a noisy room. I went upstairs. I shut the door. I was pacing like a madman. Words were pouring out of my mouth. "What the *hell* does he think he's doing! What the goddamned *hell* does he think he's doing! How could he just *come* here like this? I don't under*stand* it! What does she see in him? I can't understand it! Oh, *Christ,* what is the matter with me?" I was pacing furiously. "She *doesn't* want you! Can't you get that through your head, Swinburne? She *doesn't* want you! *She never has.* It's so goddamned pathetic. It's so goddamned humiliating." I grabbed a pillow, and I clenched it in my fists. "Why don't you wake *up!* Why don't you open your eyes? *She's in love with somebody else!*" I was screaming in a whisper. My voice was breaking. "She doesn't know you're alive. Can't you *get* that through your head! You're *nothing* to her."

I sat on the bed and cried.

She was in love with somebody else.

I splashed cold water on my face. I was still crying. I held my hands to my eyes, and I paced around the room. I couldn't stop crying. I splashed more water on my face. I had to get some air.

10

I dare not look at what I have written. A week has passed. Today Leslie's mother drove Leslie, Michael, Keating, Heather, and me to the airport to say good-bye to Amy and her family.

Amy was crying.

She gave all of us a small hug as we stood by the x-ray conveyor belt in the terminal. "So long," she said to me. Her parents were wishing good-bye to Leslie's mother. They were in good spirits.

I stood a few feet back and watched this formal ritual of good-bye. All around us there were couples kissing farewell. There was a small boy with a large suitcase, waving to his father. There were glass corridors of moving people: three levels of them. The television screen flashed the departure time; Amy's flight was blinking.

Amy wore her powder-puff football jersey.

More passengers passed in a wilted haze of

travel. There was a tired-looking limousine driver standing next to me, holding a cardboard sign saying GRAY in crayon. It seemed appropriate. Outside, through the tinted corridor windows, even the sunlight seemed gray. You could hear the airplane motors outside. Two men in airline uniforms sat on a baggage truck talking.

There were more farewells. This time it was a large family saying good-bye to their shy daughter. I wondered where she was going, why she was going. If it was so sad to leave, why were they all leaving? For a dizzying second the whole airport seemed to me just a conduit of pain. People were being wrenched from their lives. All around were great waves of emotion disturbing the air. A phrase came to my lips: *the turbulence of airports.* It was a sad place, and I wanted to go home.

Amy still looked beautiful. She was talking to Leslie's mother now, nodding. She held a tissue to wipe away her tears.

"Well, come on," I heard her father say.

They put their travel bags through the x-ray machine. Amy walked through the metal detector and the bell rang. She took out her wallet and her change and placed them in a black plastic cup. It still rang. She was half-laughing, half-crying — beautiful even in her sadness and confusion. She removed her tiny silver chain. She bent her head down, tossed her hair to the side, and found the clasp.

I watched from a distance. There was the

stately line to her neck that I had always loved, and it was caressed now by her short, straight hair. There was something in the removal of the chain that seemed to me like a purification.

I turned away to remember that final image of Amy Hart.

I could hear more fumbling with the metal detector, but I couldn't bear to look. I stared out the window at the baggage handlers.

We trooped back to the car. There was some conversation, but I wasn't listening. We were all jammed in the back of the car. The crush of bodies was somewhat amusing. I was squashed by the window, pressed next to Leslie Shapiro.

I commented that I liked her shoes. She was wearing Indian moccasins.

"They're new," she said.

I spoke without thinking. "Do you want to go to the movies tonight?" I asked.

She looked at me carefully. She had brown eyes.

"What's playing?"

I thought a moment for a good title.

"The Turbulence of Airports."

"What's that about?" she asked seriously. "I've never heard of that."

"Well," I began, "it's a long story."

O gentle reader, I knew I would always love Amy Hart. But life goes on.